NO NAMES ON THEIR GRAVES

No Names On Their Graves

by

Geoffrey Davison

Dales Large Print Books
Long Preston, North Yorkshire,
BD23 4ND, England.

British Library Cataloguing in Publication Data.

Davison, Geoffrey
　　No names on their graves.

　　A catalogue record of this book is
　　available from the British Library

　　ISBN　978-1-84262-805-8 pbk

First published in Great Britain in 1978 by Robert Hale

Copyright © Geoffrey Davison 1978

Cover illustration © Margie Hurwich by arrangement with
Arcangel Images

The moral right of the author has been asserted

Published in Large Print 2011 by arrangement with
Geoffrey Davison, care of Watson, Little Ltd.

Dales Large Print is an imprint of Library Magna Books Ltd.

Printed and bound in Great Britain by
T.J. (International) Ltd., Cornwall, PL28 8RW

The French Foreign Legion still attracts a variety of nationals to its ranks for a variety of reasons, and it still sees combat. *No Names On Their Graves* is a story about today's French Foreign Legion.

INTRODUCTION

It was early morning. A wisp of white mist hung over the plain that surrounded the small, mobile hospital unit, like the tranquil water of a lake. In the background were the mountains that separated Ethiopia from French Somaliland with their peaks reaching far into the clear, blue sky. Soon the sun would come rolling over the top of those mountains bringing the burning heat that had already parched and baked the surrounding countryside and caused famine and disease, but until then a feeling of freshness and serenity hung over the area. The native children, who lay on their beds in the open, laughed and talked cheerfully, and their voices were part of the morning freshness. The hospital staff went quickly about their business before being driven into the shade by the heat of the sun. Suddenly, the children's voices became silent. The staff were immediately attracted by this sudden change. They saw the children looking across the plain towards the mountains, where the figure of a man could be seen walking towards them. He was a tall, khaki-clad figure, and he walked with a slow, staggered gait, as

9

if every step was laboured and painful to him. Suddenly, he lurched forward and fell to the ground. The children gave a gasp and waited for him to get up. But the man didn't move. An authoritative voice called out and two Somali assistants ran out of the hospital camp in the direction of the fallen figure. They were followed by two Europeans. The party brought the man back to the hospital and took him to one of the hospital tents. Those who attended to him saw his short, sandy coloured hair and beard; his deeply tanned face with a burn mark on his cheek, and the effects of the sun on his mouth and tongue. They also saw his military type of garb and the wound on his arm.

The man lay unconscious – physically spent and suffering from the effect of the sun. The hospital staff attended to his wounds and set about nursing him back to health. For two days and two nights, he lay in a semi-conscious and delirious state, with a saline drip. Occasionally, he would call out in French, other times it would be in English. His cries were names and incoherent remarks that the staff could not interpret, but which made the man twist and turn as if in pain. The staff had a shrewd idea where he had come from and how he had got his wounds. They had heard rumours of a bloody battle between a band of native revolutionaries and French troops close to the border, but they made little reference to it amongst themselves. They were an international medical unit – a band of people dedicated to helping the suffering. The man needed their help and that was all that mattered. On the third day, the man fully recovered consciousness, but lay weak and exhausted on his bed. He spoke little to either the nursing staff, or to the doctors who attended to him.

On the fourth day, he was well enough to get out of bed. He sat in a chair, in the shade, and faced the mountains. The doctor in charge of the unit spoke to him.

'Good morning,' he said in French. 'I understand that you are a lot better today.'

'Yes, thank you,' the man replied, and added, 'I speak English. I understand that you are English.'

'Yes I am,' the doctor said. 'Are you also English?'

'No. I am American.'

'An American! Well, fortunately we speak the same language.'

'Yes.'

'Can we help you further?' the doctor asked.

'I would like to get to the American Embassy in Addis Ababa as soon as possible,' the man replied.

'There is an ambulance going there in two days' time,' the doctor explained. 'You should be fit enough to travel by then.'

'Thank you.'

'Well, that's settled. Just you rest yourself.'

The American looked at the doctor.

'I am an ex-legionnaire,' he said. 'From over the border.'

'I assumed as much,' the doctor said, 'but we don't worry about things like that. You just pull yourself together.'

'I am very grateful.'

The doctor smiled and went about his business. The American turned his attention back to the mountains from where he had come and sat staring at their distant peaks. He sat facing them all that day and all the following day. He spoke little. He was content just to sit with his own thoughts, and look at the mountains...

ONE

'Debout! Debout!'
The Corporal shouted the order that got the men out of their beds. Lee Cato stirred immediately. So did the other forty men in the barrack room. To have disobeyed would have brought instant reprisals. The men had learned the hard way. They were in the Citadel at Bonifacio, Corsica – a training camp of the Foreign Legion – and all orders had to be obeyed immediately. The men were in the final week of initial training. They had spent three months in the Citadel at Corte, and had been sent to Bonifacio to complete their training. They had been stripped of their civilian past. They were Legionnaires Second Class – men without privileges. Men to be beaten into submission – drilled to act on orders. Men not allowed to think, just to obey.

It was four a.m. Another day had started. Cato instantly shut his private thoughts behind a door in his mind. He knew that to survive, he had to obey. To be part of the machine. He became one of the forty men. He immediately set about his tasks. There was no talking, or smoking – they were not allowed. He first checked that he had his rifle charger. To lose it would mean severe punishment. He then set about making his bed, tidying his locker, laying out his uniform and polishing his area of flooring.

Everything had to be immaculate, especially the floor. He rubbed and polished it with special care. He had come to hate it. It was always there and always to be polished. And it was the Corporals' particular delight. They watched over the men as they worked on it and if they saw something they didn't like, or if they were feeling in a foul mood, they let it be known – usually with their boot. One way was to stand on the fingers of their unfortunate victim.

Someone bumped into a man carrying a steel helmet full of urine. There was a scuffle. A Corporal intervened. One of the men fell to the floor. Cato took no notice. He had seen it all before. He got on with his tasks. There could be an inspection that night. The Corporals walked up and down amongst the men, shouting abuse and smacking their batons, menacingly, against the iron bed frames. Cato washed and shaved in cold water and dressed. He checked and prepared his equipment. He kept to a drill. So did the other men. The Corporals watched them. Something didn't please one of the Corporals. He dished out his own punishment.

The bugle sounded assembly.

'R'assemblement!' came the call. *'R'assemblement!'*

Cato and the other men moved swiftly. They rushed down the iron staircase and on to the parade ground. The Sergeants and Corporals were waiting for them. Another training day was about to begin. As they paraded, a deserter was being brought back into the fortress for punishment. He looked as if he had already suffered.

'No one gets away from Bonifacio!' a Sergeant shouted.

The parade performed its daily drill and the men were marched to the gates. The order came to sing – the men sang. The Sergeants walked beside them to make sure. The men had learned the words of the songs in the barracks. Line by line the words had been beaten into them. They marched the seven kilometres to the rifle range. At the range they were detailed into firing parties. The men fired their rounds. One legionnaire was firing badly. A Sergeant dragged him, bodily, from his firing position and hit him. The man was pushed back into line. He took more care. At nine-thirty the order came to cease firing. They were taken to the sea for a swim. They bathed, naked, and ran back to the range and dried on the way. At ten o'clock the wagons brought their first meal. Cato ate and drank eagerly. So did the others. No one spoke – no one was allowed to. The Sergeants and Corporals watched over them.

Cato saw Sasous and moved beside him. Sasous was French – an ex-criminal from Paris. He had once been a king of the underworld, now he was a legionnaire. He and Cato had drawn closer to each other over the weeks. They had become comrades. There was a respect for each other. Cato was an American – tall, fair skinned, blue eyed, clean cut, and intelligent. He was not uncouth and he was not an animal, and neither was Sasous. Sasous was softly spoken, slow and ponderous with a wealth of worldly experience behind him. His breeding and background were different to Cato's. He had been born in the gutters of Paris and had fought to survive by being part of the underworld of crime. He had served two prison sentences, but in the harsh existence that faces a legionnaire under training, men are not concerned with backgrounds. They are drawn together because of the basic need to have a comrade. Sasous and Cato had been thrown together when they had enlisted. They became friends, and Cato had never stopped counting his good fortune. Cato had a purpose for being in the Legion and Sasous was helping him with it. Without Sasous, Cato's enlistment in the Legion could have been a disastrous act of folly. With Sasous' help, he could still fulfil his purpose. Sasous had a unique skill and cunning that had earned him a high reputation in the underworld, and he used it in the Legion. Despite the severe restrictions imposed on the men, he knew how to beat the system. He acquired cigarettes and money when others had neither, and with them he ran his own grapevine in the barracks and his own links with the outside world. He kept in touch and he kept Cato informed.

Cato wasn't the only American in the camp. There was another – a man called Vasey, by the Legion. The Legion changed all their names. Cato had been Carter. Vasey had been Vacinie. He was an ignorant, aggressive American of Italian descent, from the East end of New York. Cato had learned all about him. He had made it his business to find out. Vasey was on the run. So was the man Cato was looking for, but it wasn't Vasey. So Cato left him alone. Vasey was always in trouble. He was a slow learner and had difficulty with the French language. His difficulty showed on his face which was constantly taking a beating for his lack of understanding. Twice he had been given special treatment, but his learning rate hadn't increased. He hadn't the mentality.

Their brief respite was soon over. The men were assembled again and ordered to empty their packs and hand them to a Sergeant to be filled with rocks. The Sergeant was feeling in a foul mood that day. He had drunk too much *vino* the previous evening. He filled their packs with fifty kilos of rocks. The men mentally groaned. It was going to be another, particularly, hard day.

The training continued. With full equipment, armed, and their packs filled with rocks, they moved out. They did the short course flat out. They did the long course in a quicker time than usual. They marched, they ran, and they did infantry training amongst the gorse bushes that covered their rocky training area. They sweated and endured.

In the late afternoon they returned to the fortress. Outside the gates they formed rank. They entered the fortress singing. The Sergeants watched their performance. Any slackness, any show of weakness or fatigue, brought immediate punishment. Inside the fortress, they were paraded, and the ritual of the final parade was carried out with all its pomp and ceremony.

They were also told the fate of the man who had deserted, as a warning. He was on the *rocks*. Staked to a bed of rocks and covered with a small tent to protect him from the sun, he was to be left to dwell on his misdeed without food or water. He wouldn't die – the Legion would see to that, but he wouldn't desert again.

Cato's section was dismissed to their quarters. They moved at the double. They locked their rifles in the chains and kept their chargers. The Corporal made them assemble outside the barrack room. He told them that that night was *'poof'* night – the night they had to attend the camp brothel. Cato was pleased. He wanted information and he wanted it badly. He knew that the Madame who ran the brothel was one of Sasous' sources of information.

They were marched to the mess hall where they ate their big meal of the day and drank as much *'vino'* as they wished. Again Cato and Sasous kept together.

'Perhaps we shall learn something tonight,' Cato whispered.

Sasous sighed, and looked at Cato with a pained look on his face.

'That Madame,' he said, and gave a shudder.

'Cheer up,' Cato smiled, 'perhaps tonight she will smell of some expensive perfume instead of garlic. Or perhaps you will get one of the girls.'

Sasous gave a look that suggested he would not be so fortunate.

After the meal the men were marched back to their barracks. A song sheet was displayed on the wall. They learned another song, line by line. The Corporals marched the alleyway between the bunks and tested the men one by one. The legionnaire being tested turned his back on the Corporal and repeated the line. If he did it incorrectly, he was punched in the kidneys, or in the stomach. Some were hit. Vasey was always one of those who suffered. After the song lesson, they were assembled outside the barracks and marched to the canteen. Part of it was used as the brothel. It was run by a Madame and two girls from the town. They catered for all the needs of the men in the camp. The Madame was elderly, fat, and unappealing, but when the girls were hard pressed she would take her place in one of the rooms, and a legionnaire detailed to her had no option but to obey.

The men were paraded and waited their turn. Cato's name was called out. He stepped forward and reported, loudly, to the Sergeant.

'Legionnaire Cato! Sergeant.'

'Legionnaire Cato!' the Sergeant barked. *'Chambre Une – Poof!'*

Cato collected two green tickets and crossed to where the Madame sat beside several crates of beer. She collected the tickets, greedily, and gave him two bottles of beer. He went into room number one. The girl was lying naked on the bed waiting for him. He had seen her before. She was in her twenties – dark haired, dark skinned, with plenty to get hold of. There were beads of perspiration on her brow and a fixed smile on her lips that would fade as she went through her quota of men.

Cato *'poofed'*. Afterwards, he went into the canteen. He knocked off a bottle top and slowly drank his beer. The Legion was like a jungle, he thought – rough, crude, and animal-like, but he had expected no other and he could take it all – until he found his man. An argument suddenly broke out between two men at another table. One of the men was called Hook. He was a big, tough Dutchman. An area was instantly cleared and the two men lashed into each other. The fight lasted until two Corporals decided that it had gone on long enough. They moved in and quickly, and brutally, brought it to a close. The rest of the men settled down to their beer again. Sasous came into the canteen. He gave an amused smile, as he sat at the table opposite Cato.

'It makes a change, *mon ami*,' he said.

'The girls?' Cato asked.

There was a glint in Sasous' eye.

'No, the fight,' he suggested. He looked thoughtful. 'There must be some advantage in having a name near the top of the alphabet,' he added.

Cato smiled. 'You got the Madame?'

'I got the Madame,' Sasous agreed, 'but it was worth it.'

Cato's eyes lit up.

'You got some news, Sasous?'

'Yes.'

He leaned across the table so that he was closer to his friend. His face was serious.

'Two men purchased false papers and arranged to join the Legion at the time your man, Pedrides, went to ground,' he whispered. 'There were no others.'

Cato's spirits soared. That was the very news that he had been waiting for. That was the information that Sasous had been seeking ever since he and Cato had teamed up together in Marseilles. By *arranged* Cato knew that Sasous meant that the two men had bought their way into the Legion. They had purchased a set of papers and documents that would be acceptable to the Legion – a false background that would prevent their true identities from being traced, but which would satisfy the Legion. The Legion liked to know about its recruits – all about them. It would help them and protect them, but not if they were wanted by *Interpol*. But there were ways and means of twisting the rules, and Cato's man had done just that. Cato looked at his friend.

'That is good,' he said. 'Very good.'

'They had both come from Spain,' Sasous whispered.

That was where Cato's man had come from.

'They both fit the description of your man,' Sasous went on. 'One of them sold a Mexican passport to pay for his papers. The other had a faked Spanish passport. Their legion names are Mandril and Pescod.'

Mandril and Pescod. Cato would never forget those names. A surge of relief passed through his body. His gamble in joining the Legion was beginning to pay off.

'Where are they now?' he asked.

Sasous gave a faint smile and looked apologetic. 'In time, *mon ami*,' he said, 'in time, but do not worry. We will find your man.'

Cato gripped his friend's arm in gratitude. 'Sure,' he agreed. 'We will find him. You have done well, Sasous. Very well. Thank you.'

Sasous moved closer. He had more to tell Cato.

'Lieutenant Deval and fourteen replacements are to be posted to the Reconnaissance Regiment in Djibouti,' he said, and sat back. A party of legionnaires had joined their table.

Cato was curious to know more. He knew little about the Lieutenant. He was a young, professional officer who was in charge of their section. He was often seen watching the men from a distance – a lonely, detached figure.

'We are both to be detailed,' Sasous whispered. 'So is Sergeant Bouchier.'

Bouchier! Cato looked at his friend, sharply. Sasous gave him a sign telling him to be cautious. Cato drank his beer. Of all the

Sergeants in the Legion, Bouchier was the last one Cato wanted to serve with. Bouchier was known to him. He was known to them all. He was on the instructing staff. He was an elderly, squat, barrel shaped, bastard. A sadist who enjoyed his power over the men. He was a native of Alsace, but of German extraction, and was supposed to have served as a youth with the German Army. He always wore skin coloured gloves and carried a cane. The gloves were rumoured to cover an S.S. tattoo mark on each hand, but that had never been confirmed. His hands had never been seen without the gloves. The cane he used as a weapon to force his authority over the men. He had an expert's knowledge of the tender parts of the human body and used his cane to inflict sharp, seething stabs of pain on his victims.

The Lieutenant was still an unknown. Bouchier wasn't.

'You have heard nothing,' Sasous whispered. 'Not even the Lieutenant knows.'

Cato gave a wry smile. 'It has been decided?' he asked.

'It will be tomorrow,' Sasous replied.

'And what about those other two men?' Cato asked. 'Could they be in East Africa?'

'They could,' Sasous agreed. 'There are not many postings abroad. We will find out when we are in Corte.'

Cato's hand gripped his bottle of beer. His

man just had to be in Djibouti, he thought grimly. He just had to be.

'And if he isn't,' Sasous said, 'then we can request a transfer posting. We will find him.'

Cato relaxed. They were making progress and that was important.

'Sure, Sasous,' he said. 'Sure.'

At nine p.m. Cato and the others were in their beds. Cato closed his eyes and welcomed the thought of sleep. In sleep he was at peace with himself. But sleep didn't come that night. Sasous had told him of two men. Two men who had joined the Legion at the same time, and in the same way, as the man Cato was looking for. That was enough to prevent him from sleeping. He had got the scent of his goal. He opened his eyes and stared at the ceiling above him. The old would had been opened up. It was all with him again, but in his thoughts he wasn't Lee Cato, Legionnaire Second Class, a man drilled into submission. He was Lee Carter, the family man. The man with a wife and a son. Lee Carter, the Architect. A man who was going places, until his world had suddenly come to an end one wet, November afternoon, in a bank in Philadelphia. He could see it all quite clearly – the large, marble panelled hall of the bank; the startled looks on the faces of the bank officials, and the black masked faces of the gangsters with their sub machine guns. He could hear the sudden cries of panic and fright of the people in the bank; the sharp, abrupt orders from the gangsters and the immediate response from the officials. He could also hear the raiders running through the cubicled rooms shouting orders to each other and see them scurrying to the exit with their bags of money. And he could see the small, slim, black clothed figure of the *bomber* leaning casually against a marble pillar with a toy-like object in his hand. He had been the last of the raiders to leave the bank and he had passed so close to where Cato had been standing that Cato had looked into his cold, grey eyes. There had been one fleeting moment when Cato thought of trying to overpower him, but he had held back for fear of reprisals from the rest of the gang and the opportunity had passed. The man had moved away from him and ran to the exit. For a moment, he had just stood in the doorway, then he had casually thrown his toy at a group of innocent bystanders. Only his toy had been a bomb and Cato's family had been some of the bystanders.

Cato clenched his fists and stared at the ceiling. The pain gripped his body and made him perspire. He could see and feel it all. The scene in the bank, the interviews with the F.B.I. men and the days that had followed. They were all there on the rough concrete ceiling in front of him like a film at a movie show. It had happened before and it would happen again, and he didn't want to stop it. He wanted to remember.

The F.B.I had been polite. They had even appeared concerned, but their concern was superficial. Their handshakes were meaningless gestures that lacked sincerity. Their sharp actions and quick interchange of orders and cryptic messages were a repeat from other similar incidents. They had seen it all before, and their progress was slow – very slow, but finally they had made some arrests.

Ryder, who was in charge of the F.B.I. investigation, explained about the arrests to Carter.

'The gang that raided the bank,' he said, 'are a self styled Freedom Liberation Group. They are a mixed group of men and women, in their early twenties. Some are known Communists, others are anarchists, and some just dropouts. They have a Robin Hood concept. They distribute their takings in the slum quarters of the city.'

Carter had known all this. It had been in every newspaper in the country, if not in the world. It had been news for three days. It was then history, three months old.

'Yesterday we arrested five of the group,' Ryder went on. 'We picked up their trail in

New Orleans. Two of them were shot, dead. The five will stand trial. It will be in the press tonight.'

'And the man who threw the bomb at my family?' Carter asked. 'Black beard?'

'He fled the country about two months ago,' Ryder frowned. 'He is somewhere in Europe.'

'Somewhere in Europe?'

'We have been in touch with Interpol,' Ryder explained. 'He landed in Spain – Madrid. He has not been seen since. We have several contacts and agencies looking for him.'

'I see.'

'I don't want to fool you. Things look bad.'

'What do you mean, things look bad? Spell it out.'

'They picked up a lead in Marseilles and lost it. The guy has disappeared.'

'A guy just can't disappear,' Carter snapped.

'Marseilles is not the States,' Ryder replied. 'We are dealing with a country that is...' He shrugged as he looked for the right words. 'Well, let's say they are not one hundred per cent sympathetic towards us. They have their own problems.'

'They're covering up, or something?' Carter asked.

'No,' Ryder said. 'I think that they just don't want to turn over too many stones.'

'Meaning?'

'I have a hunch that the guy joined the Foreign Legion. I also have a hunch that they don't want to admit it.'

'Foreign Legion!' Carter growled. 'My God, this is the seventies. Their Legion is not some escape from justice.'

'Not any longer,' Ryder agreed, 'but they still accept a lot of undesirables. It is still a kind of sanctuary.'

Carter smoked a cigarette. The Foreign Legion! He knew a bit about it. He had read about it in books and magazines.

'The Legion does not accept criminals,' he said. 'They also recognise extradition rights.'

Ryder held up his hands in protest.

'O.K., O.K.,' he said. 'I know the score.'

'Well, the guy who murdered my family can't just go joining the Legion,' Carter fumed.

'Yes, he can,' Ryder said.

Carter shook his head in disgust.

'Let's just look at some facts again,' Ryder said. 'The guy gave his name as Gus Pedrides. That is the only name the group knew him by, but there is no record anywhere of a Gus Pedrides, so he could have been an illegal immigrant to the States from anywhere. The group picked him up in the back streets of New Orleans. He was a slim, dark haired guy about five foot seven inches tall and weighed about one hundred and fifty pounds. He had a heavy, black beard and grey eyes. He was about twenty-three years of age. Perhaps from a French background. He could speak French. We have nothing on him – no police record – no fingerprints, and no photograph other than the identity kit impression, but take off the beard and you've got another identity, and another guy.'

'How about mannerisms, attitudes?'

'He was a quiet guy, who wore a grudge against society on his shoulder the size of a plank. Somewhere along the line something had gone wrong. He said little. He had just dropped out and lived from the gutter. The group let him tag along. Their motives were not all violent. Some of them actually believe in their crap. They did give money away.'

Carter breathed heavily and clenched his fists in anger.

'We have nothing to give the French Sûreté to work on,' Ryder went on. 'Only a description that would probably fit a hundred other guys, and if Pedrides is smart, he will have prepared his alibi.'

'You might pick up a fingerprint from somewhere,' Carter insisted.

Ryder shrugged. 'We might,' he agreed, 'but it is unlikely.'

Carter looked glum. 'How come you think

he is in the Legion?' he asked.

'We followed his trail to Marseilles, to a contact who is well known for preparing the way for people to get into the Legion. This contact operates a kind of black market form of recruiting service. He provides a false set of personal details and papers which the authorities will accept.'

'Is there nothing you have to help pin him down?'

Ryder looked sullen.

'We have nothing so far. We are working on the group. They might come up with something. If we get anything to fix him, we'll put pressure on the French to make a move.' He shrugged. 'I still don't promise anything.'

Carter had drank himself to sleep that night. He was steamed up. It wasn't the Legion or the French. It was the fact that the man who had killed his family had escaped the net and was still free. The following day he took the car close to the point at Little Creek. It was where he had always brought his family for a day at the sea. The breeze was fresh; the sea was riding high. The beach was deserted. He started walking. In the back of his mind was the idea of going after the killer himself. To join the Legion. He was not a young man, but he was still a fit one. But that didn't come into it. What mattered was his peace of mind, and he knew that he would never get that by trying to pick up the loose threads and carry on as if everything was normal. He was a man in a vacuum. He was lost. He needed a cause and so long as Pedrides was free, he could be that cause. The idea to go after Pedrides fermented in his mind and began to take root. Finally it got a grip on him. He would go looking for Pedrides in the Legion. If he was there, he would come across him – somewhere, and sometime.

The smell of urine irritated Cato's nostrils. He looked away from the concrete ceiling. The man from the bunk below him was relieving himself into his steel helmet. Cato turned his back on him. He was a legionnaire, second class, again, but he had his purpose, and it kept him going. He closed his eyes and fell asleep.

TWO

Lieutenant Paul Deval stood aloof and alone on the rifle range watching the Sergeants drill the men. He was a slim, youthful-looking officer of medium height with sharp, aristocratic features and a confident manner that came from the knowledge that he had a wealthy and influential family behind him. His father owned a chain of newspapers with its head office in Paris. His brother was a member of the Assembly, and his uncle was a General on the Military Staff. The three together formed a powerful triumvirate to help and promote the younger Deval with his career and, like the rest of his family, he was very ambitious to succeed. He had passed through the Military Academy at St Cyr with flying colours. He had selected to serve with the Legion only because it was potentially the most promising unit for him to attract attention to himself. He intended to use the Legion as a stepping stone in his career, but he had tired of the routine of the Corsican training camp. He wanted to be away from it, and he wanted action – some minor military success that he could get his family to capitalise on. In East Africa, in the

French territory of Afars and Issas, there was internal trouble and there was bush warfare on its borders. The Legion was regularly involved. That was where Deval wanted to be, and with his uncle's influence, that was where he was being sent. As he stood on the range, he was patiently contemplating his future posting and his future successes. Failure never entered his head. He had inherited his family's belief in their divine right to high office, along with their ability to wheel and deal and bend the rules to suit their own purpose. He had also inherited their liking of power, but his own particular liking was not on the same scale as his father's, or his brother's. He was not seeking power in the major leagues. His likeness for power was more personal and more detailed. He liked to influence people and see their reaction. To him, the legionnaires under his command were pawns in his game of life, and over the months of watching them he had picked the pawns that interested him the most. He knew quite a lot about some of the men under his command. More than any of them realised.

An orderly came up to him on the range, saluted, and told him that he was requested to report to the Camp Administration Officer, immediately. He acknowledged the message, and knew that his plans were beginning to take shape. He returned to the

Citadel and entered the administration block. The Administration Officer, Lieutenant Corvette, was seated at his desk when Deval entered his room. He was an older man than Deval and had long since been passed over in the promotion race. It had made him cynical and suspicious of ambitious, Academy trained officers, and with Deval, he had the added distaste of knowing that the rules and customs of the Legion were being bent to suit Deval's wishes.

'I have a message for you,' he said. 'Mademoiselle Chauvier has arrived at her hotel.'

'Thank you,' Deval replied. 'I was expecting Mademoiselle Chauvier. She is a friend.'

'I hope I will have the pleasure of meeting her,' Lieutenant Corvette remarked.

'I am sure you will.'

'Is she here on holiday?'

'On holiday,' Deval agreed.

The subject passed to the day's training. Corvette was making Deval wait before informing him of his posting. Deval was patient. He already knew what he was to be told. His uncle had written to him giving him the facts.

'Your request has been approved,' Corvette said finally. 'You are to report to the 3rd Reconnaissance Regiment, in Djibouti, with a section of men as replacement for their losses.'

Deval's face remained straight, but his eyes gave the faintest suspicion of a glitter of satisfaction.

'Sergeant Bouchier has also been detailed to go with you. He has been informed.'

Deval raised an eyebrow. 'Sergeant Bouchier?'

'He can be relied upon in action. He requested the posting.'

Deval made no further comment. He knew all about Bouchier.

'And the men?'

Corvette handed him a typed list. Deval read the names. A smile appeared on his lips. Some of the men who particularly interested him appeared on the list. One of them was the American, Cato. He handed the list back to Corvette.

'Are they to be informed?' he asked.

'Yes. Sergeant Bouchier will tell them, if they haven't already heard on their grapevine.'

'When do we leave?'

'As soon as the men complete their training and return to Corte. Probably next week.'

'Good.'

Corvette glanced at some papers on his desk. Deval knew that he was being dismissed.

'You may carry on, Monsieur,' Corvette remarked.

Deval saluted and left the office.

For a while Corvette sat deep in thought, then he got up from his desk and went into the office of the 'Captain of the Legion'. The Captain looked up at him.

'I have just spoken to Deval, *mon Capitaine,*' Corvette said.

The Captain sat back. He had already recognised the Lieutenant's dislike of the young officer.

'Deval is very ambitious,' he said. 'He has used his influence and family connections to get this posting. He wants some action.'

'Yes, *mon Capitaine.*'

'You might not like Deval,' the Captain said, 'and I certainly don't like this double dealing behind our backs, but *mon Dieu!* it goes on all the time. If I had Deval's connections I would be a Marshal of France by now.'

'Quite,' the Lieutenant agreed.

'Deval is out to prove himself,' the Captain went on. 'He has to live up to the family tradition. He is scratching around for an opportunity to get some glory. He might get a shock instead.' He turned his attention back to his papers. 'Deval should have been born earlier,' he added, as final judgment on the man. 'He should have fought in the war.'

'Yes,' the Lieutenant agreed. 'He missed both Indo-China and Algeria.'

'I was thinking in particular of the last World War,' the Captain added.

The Lieutenant sighed. 'I wonder which side he would have fought on?' he asked, and left the room before the Captain could take him to task on the question.

Deval left the administrative block, totally unconcerned about Corvette's resentment of his posting. He had long since been able to divorce himself from any peripheral upsets that his actions might cause. He was totally dedicated to his ambitions. He saw Sergeant Bouchier waiting for the men to return from the training range. He called to him. The Sergeant marched over to where Deval was standing and saluted, respectfully. The two men stood facing each other. They were of similar height, but that was the only likeness. Deval was youthful, slim with light hazel eyes, thin narrow lips, and a tanned, aristocratic face. He was a gentleman and he was cultured. Bouchier was rough, coarse, and aggressive, with a face that was scarred and marked. He was not a young man, but he was a fit one, and what he lost in years he made up for in experience.

'I understand that we are to serve together,' Deval remarked.

'Yes, *mon Lieutenant.*'

'You requested the posting, Sergeant. Why?'

'There is a lot of fighting going on in the

territory, *mon Lieutenant.* I prefer to be with the action.'

Deval's eyes lit up.

'Good, Sergeant,' he said. 'Very good. And what about the men?'

Bouchier scowled.

'They are the scum from the bottom of the barrel, *mon Lieutenant,* but they will not let you down.'

'*Bien,*' Deval said. 'We shall see.'

He walked away and left the Sergeant to await the return of the men. He felt pleased that Bouchier was to serve with him. Bouchier had the right attitude for Deval.

THREE

Cato and the men returned to the Citadel. The Sergeants addressed their respective sections.

'When the parade is dismissed,' one of them shouted, 'the following men will stand fast.' He called out some names. The other section N.C.O.'s were doing the same. Cato's name was called. So was Sasous'.

'*Guarde à vous*,' came the order and the parade came to attention. The parade was presented to the Senior Officer by the Sergeant Adjutant and the traditional ceremony of passing the parade down the ranks took place. Finally the parade was dismissed. The men went to their barracks at the double, except Cato and the other men whose names had been called out. They stood rigidly to attention at irregular intervals around the parade ground. Twelve legionnaires and one Corporal.

For a full two minutes nothing happened. The men remained standing to attention with their equipment on their backs and their rifles slung over their shoulders. Not one dared to move. None of them knew what to expect.

Finally, Sergeant Bouchier made his appearance. First, he stood at the edge of the parade ground silently willing one of the standing figures to glance in his direction, then he marched into the middle of the parade ground so that they could all see him. He was like an actor squeezing every theatrical ounce of advantage out of his entrance. He stood in the middle of the square, smacking his cane against the palm of his left hand and scowling at the men around him. Then he marched to where the Corporal – Corporal Schnell – was standing to attention. The Corporal saluted him. The Sergeant returned the salute and made a slight movement with his cane. The Corporal understood. He saluted again and turned to face the men.

'*R'assemblement!*' he shouted.

Cato and the others quickly aligned themselves in front of the Corporal. The Corporal brought them to attention and presented them to the Sergeant. Bouchier acknowledged the salute and stood smacking the cane against his hand. He slowly surveyed the line of men, his mouth twisting in a sneering smile, which the men only sensed. Their eyes were rigidly fixed on the yellow walls in the background. They knew Bouchier, and they knew his tactics.

'You scum have been selected for posting to the Reconnaissance Regiment in Djibouti,' he hissed. He eyed them menacingly. 'You will be serving with me,' he barked. 'We will be together.' Again he surveyed the line. 'Why have you been selected?' he asked. He didn't expect an answer and he didn't get one. 'I will tell you,' he said. There was a moment's pause. 'You are the scum of the Legion,' he hissed, 'and you need my special care and attention.'

His raucous voice carried across the deserted parade ground for all to hear. He surveyed the line with disgust for a full minute and then he walked to the end of the line, where Cato was standing. Cato stood rigidly to attention, his eyes staring into the distance above Bouchier's shoulder.

'Cato,' Bouchier grinned. He knew Cato and he knew that Cato was intelligent, and he didn't like the type. They could out-think him. He preferred the crooks, smugglers, and the other cast-outs. Those he understood and could bully. He also liked to know about the men's past, and he knew nothing about Cato.

'I hope you get some intelligent conversation from this scum,' he snarled, and flicked his cane into Cato's side. Cato felt the pain surge through his body and mentally cursed the Sergeant.

Bouchier moved to the next man – a tall, solid looking Dutchman.

'Hook,' he hissed.

42

Hook was not the Dutchman's *nom de guerre,* but it was the name that he was called because it was well known that he had killed a man with a large, iron hook. A technicality of the law had saved him from a long prison sentence, but not from his fellow men. Now he was in the Legion.

Bouchier gave a snort of delight. The Dutchman was coarse and animal-like, and he took a delight in dealing with his kind.

'Hook,' he hissed again. 'We'll see just how tough you really are – eh *cochon?*'

He sank his fist into the Dutchman's stomach, but the man's stomach muscles were like iron. He didn't move, but his eyes blazed with anger. Bouchier saw them and laughed. He moved to the next man – another of the same type as the Dutchman. This man was a Belgian. His name was Boussec, and he had also killed a man. He had worked in a meat factory where one day he had gone berserk and killed one of his fellow workmen in a fight. He had spent several years in gaol before joining the Legion.

'Ah! Boussec and Hook together,' Bouchier said. 'Well now that is appropriate.' He gave a snort and prodded the man's stomach with the end of his cane. 'Still overweight,' he hissed. 'We will have to do something about that.' He looked into the man's face which was perspiring. It was a rough, red, flabby face. Beads of perspiration were rolling down the cheeks.

'Won't we, Boussec?' he sneered, and suddenly sank his fist into the man's stomach. Boussec's eyes looked as if they were going to pop out of their sockets. His mouth opened wide and he stifled a groan, but he stayed on his feet.

'See to it,' Bouchier added and moved to the next man. He was of the same height as Bouchier. A man with a dark, handsome face, and dark, flashing eyes. He was a Greek – a revolutionary who had fallen foul of his Government. Greco was his *nom de guerre*.

'Greco,' Bouchier said with less contempt than he had given Boussec, but he still flicked his cane with gusto into the man's stomach. At the same time he looked into the Greek's dark eyes and saw the silent resistance and hatred in them. He gave a satisfied smirk.

'So you do not like me?' he taunted, and the cane flicked into the Greek's side again. 'What are you going to do about it? Eh, Greco?' He gave a deep chuckle of delight.

The Greek made no answer. To have done so would have given Bouchier an excuse for a further demonstration of his power over them.

'You'll do nothing,' Bouchier smirked. 'You are like all the rest – all talk.'

He went to the next legionnaire – a round faced, tanned German.

'Hessler,' he said. Again the cane whip-lashed into the man's stomach.

'Still not sleeping at nights?' he asked secretively, but in a voice that all the men on the parade ground could hear. 'Who are you waiting for, Hessler?' he asked and gave a chuckle of delight. Hessler was known to lie all night with his eyes open. 'A woman?' he sneered. 'Or is someone going to murder you?'

He didn't wait for an answer. He went to the next man in the line – a solid looking man of medium height with broad shoulders, a powerful chest, and a rough boxer's face. It was Vasey, the only other American in the Citadel, besides Cato.

'Mon Dieu!' Bouchier hissed. 'Vasey! We are scraping the bottom of the barrel.' His cane came to rest on Vasey's stomach with more force than he had previously used. He despised Vasey, partly because he detested all Americans and partly because of Vasey's inability to master the basic French words of command.

'You and Cato will be able to have some cosy chats about home,' he sneered, and gave a deep chuckle of delight. The thought of Cato and Vasey sitting talking together appealed to his sense of humour. He laughed loudly.

'What do you think of that, Cato?' he called out. He got no answer from Cato, and Vasey hadn't even understood what Bouchier was talking about. Bouchier realised that and flicked his cane into the lower part of Vasey's body where it hurt most. Vasey's eyes watered with the sharp, piercing pain, but he stood his ground.

'*Cochon!*' Bouchier spat, and went to the next man.

'Irish!' he exclaimed.

The man in front of him was a middle-aged man with flashing, furtive eyes and a nervous twitch of his nose. Like the rest of the men of the section, he was tanned and stripped of any civilian appearance. His name was Riley, but to Bouchier he was Irish.

'Still sleeping badly, Irish?' Bouchier sneered. He knew that Irish had nightmares and often called out in his sleep, and he had a shrewd idea what troubled him.

Irish looked straight past the Sergeant.

'You had better be careful,' Bouchier hissed. 'Hessler doesn't sleep at all at nights. He might also learn what troubles you so.'

The cane sank into the Irishman's stomach. The Irishman forced himself not to react. He gripped the butt of his rifle and wished the Sergeant into hell. Bouchier hit him again and went to the next man. He was the smallest legionnaire in the line. A stocky, dark faced man with dark, nervous eyes. He was a Corsican and Bouchier had already nicknamed him Napoleon.

'Ah! Napoleon,' he said and prodded the man's stomach. 'Still waiting for your Corsican brothers to catch up with you?' he asked.

The Corsican didn't move. He braced his stomach muscles and waited for the cane to make contact. He didn't have to wait long. Bouchier lashed into him.

'Still enjoying the *poofing?*' Bouchier sneered.

It was well known that *poofing* was Napoleon's delight and his downfall. Napoleon thought of nothing else but *poofing,* but he had *poofed* once too often and had disgraced his family. That was why he was now in the Legion.

'You lousy peasant!' Bouchier said.

He moved along the line. The next legionnaire who confronted him was Sasous. He was tall and slim, with prominent, pointed features. Bouchier looked at him and gave a snort of disgust. He knew all about Sasous and his past, and he wasn't impressed.

'Still dreaming about Paris?' he mocked, but didn't wait for an answer. He sank his cane into Sasous' side. The Frenchman forced himself to suffer the pain without reacting. 'You won't ever see Paris again,' Bouchier said. 'So keep dreaming.' He hit

47

him again and moved along the line. He stood in front of the next legionnaire. He was the youngest legionnaire in the section. A handsome, youthful looking Swede with an evenly tanned complexion, pale blue eyes, blond hair and a fiery temper. They had met before and Bouchier suspected him of being a homosexual.

'Hello, Berge,' Bouchier said. His cane hit the Swede in the same place that it had caught Vasey, but with more force. Bouchier knew that Berge was one of the few men in the section that he could force a reaction out of.

Berge's face muscles went taut. Bouchier saw it.

'Will your friends miss you,' he sneered. Berge didn't reply. 'Or will you still be seeing them in the *slats?*'

He hit the Swede again. 'I am going to personally watch you *poof,* Berge,' he hissed. 'I want to see that you do it like all the rest – the proper way! I know your type. I have a nose for smelling them out.'

Berge moved his head as if in defiance of the Sergeant's remarks. Bouchier saw it and brought his fist into the man's stomach with so much force that it made the man double up. Bouchier immediately grabbed him and held him upright. The young Swede was choking for breath.

'Nobody falls!' Bouchier shouted. 'Nobody even moves,' he added, 'unless I give the order!'

Berge got his breath back.

'Remember that, legionnaire,' he warned. He moved to the next man. He was another German. A serious faced, quiet man, of medium build.

'Fritz,' Bouchier said, giving the man a new nickname. He flicked the cane into the man's stomach, but he knew that the German wouldn't be drawn. He knew the man was too full of hatred for himself to show any outward feeling. It was all inside him, just as it was with Cato. He stood silently cursing the man. He knew very little about Fritz except that he had come from East Germany where he was supposed to have been in a position of authority. He grunted and hit the German again just for the hell of it, but the German took it as he seemed to take everything about the Legion – as a penance.

Bouchier moved to the next legionnaire. It was Diago, the Spaniard – a small, dark, swarthy man, with a constant scowl on his face. Diago was someone Bouchier did know about – everybody knew about him. He wore his hatred on his sleeve. He hated the Fascists who had expelled him from his country, and it occupied his thoughts and conversation constantly.

Bouchier looked at him thoughtfully.

Diago was another Greco, he thought. They were supposed to be two of a kind, but they had kept their distance. There was something between the two men that made them mistrust each other.

'Still playing with the knife,' Bouchier hissed. Diago was also known for his love of his knives, which he cleaned and played with like a child with a toy.

Diago didn't reply. Bouchier hit him in the stomach and the hatred showed in Diago's eyes.

'You wouldn't dare, Diago,' Bouchier snarled.

He turned his back on the men and walked up to Corporal Schnell. The Corporal had already completed two tours of duty. He was a German – a big, well-made man who spoke little. He was the ideal legionnaire – strong, fit and not too intelligent. He obeyed orders without question – all orders.

'Corporal Schnell,' Bouchier said, and tapped the Corporal gently on the shoulder with his cane. 'Good.' he added. The Corporal had served in Algeria with Bouchier when the Legion had been stationed at Sidi bel Abbes. It had been a dirty, back-stabbing campaign – but Corporal Schnell always obeyed orders...

'So,' Bouchier said, and gave a knowing smile.

Abruptly, he swung around on his heels

and faced the line of men.

'From now on, I will be with you. I will not disappoint you. You had better not disappoint me.'

He turned and marched smartly off the parade ground.

The men didn't relax. The Corporals were almost as powerful as the Sergeants, and Corporal Schnell was an unknown factor to them. Schnell waited until Bouchier was out of sight and then dismissed them.

'*Merde!*' Diago hissed, as they broke ranks. 'We have got a right bastard with that Sergeant.'

Cato looked at Sasous. Sasous returned the look with a shrug and shake of his head. They both agreed with Diago.

'Move it!' Corporal Schnell shouted. '*Pronto!*'

FOUR

Jaquie Chauvier waited for Lieutenant Deval to join her at her hotel. She had arrived from Paris that morning at Deval's invitation, and it was her first visit to Bonifacio. The town interested her. She sat on her balcony and studied the lights of the harbour and the old town that stood high on a promontory, with the floodlit garrison fortress within its walls. The atmosphere of the thirteenth century town probably hadn't changed much over the years, she thought. It was still there – dark, cool and mysterious, and the Legion fitted into it ideally. It had brought the scent of Africa and adventure with it. She was glad she had come, she thought. When Deval had invited her she had been uncertain. Now she was glad. She had a feeling that life had turned over another page for her. There was a challenge about her visit, and her assignment to Djibouti, that she had needed in her life.

There was a knock on her bedroom door, and Deval joined her. He looked tanned and fit. The Legion was suiting him, she thought. He stood smiling at her with his arms outstretched.

'Jaquie, darling,' he said. 'It is nice to see you again.'

They embraced.

'You look more attractive each time I see you,' he said, and stood apart from her and looked at her. There was a lot about Jaquie that he liked. She was young, attractive, shapely, and intelligent. She had made her own mark in the newspaper world, but had still kept her feminine charm and appeal. She had most of the qualities that Deval liked in a woman, but Deval didn't want a woman, and he didn't want Jaquie. They knew each other too well.

They stood on the balcony. Deval poured out some drinks.

'What do you think of the place?' he asked, waving his hand at the town.

'You can almost touch its atmosphere,' she said, 'and the fortress certainly looks very impregnable.'

'From the outside to get in,' he replied, 'and from the inside to get out.'

'What will the legionnaires be doing now?'

'Sleeping. They have been exercised, fed and watered. They're now asleep.'

'You make them sound like animals.'

'Human animals,' he replied, with a smile.

Jaquie wrapped her arms around herself. She had suddenly felt a chill in the night air. It was as if Deval's remark had reminded her of something she had forgotten about him. She didn't like his remark. It had sounded indecent. She had become interested in the Legion after Deval had got his father's records department to probe into some of his men. She had suddenly become aware that the Legion still existed, and she had become interested in the men. They were not just pawns to her.

Deval took her hand.

'Thank you for researching that information for me,' he said, 'and for coming.'

She looked away. 'It was not my doing,' she said. 'It was your father's instructions. The challenge amused him. His records department did the rest.'

Deval chuckled his delight.

'I thought it would. How is he these days?'

'He is very well. Just the same.' She shrugged. 'Perhaps a little worried about your motives.' She looked serious. 'Why did you really want to know about those men?' she asked.

Deval sat back. 'They interested me,' he said. 'Especially Carter. He stuck out like a sore thumb.'

'Ah, Carter,' Jaquie said. She knew about Carter.

'Carter, the romantic American,' Deval laughed. 'It is not very often that we get an American in the Legion, and especially not an educated one. It is natural that I should be curious about him.'

'And now that you know about him. What do you think?'

'The man is either a fool chasing a wild dream, or a man of courage after revenge.'

'Which one is it?'

Deval shook his head. 'We shall see,' he said. 'He is one of the fourteen murderers and cut throats that I am taking to East Africa with me. We will see how he reacts when he comes face to face with death.'

Jaquie turned on him.

'Don't talk like that,' she said. 'Don't even think like that.'

'Why not?' he asked. 'We have lost twenty men in the last month in the territory. There is heavy fighting in the hills. The Russians are supporting the revolutionaries and encouraging them to incite the natives to fight against our Government. Everybody knows what is going on even if the press is keeping it at a low key. The territory is a cauldron of unrest.'

'And if there is an opportunity for you to fight them you will welcome it,' she said.

'But of course. I am a professional soldier.'

Jaquie frowned. There was something very familiar about Deval's remarks and the events that he was forecasting. It was as if she had lived them, or dreamed them, all before. All at once she felt like a person standing in the wings of a stage watching a play, that she knew, being enacted. She could see Deval in Africa. She could see him in action with his men. She could see it all – except the ending. It was as if her dream had faded away and never ended. She stood up and went to the balcony rail. She had thought that the invitation to go to Djibouti had been a challenge to her – a stimulant to her life. Something to excite her – to interest her. Now she was beginning to wonder if it wasn't part of her destiny. The excitement she had felt about her assignment had left her. She was being sent to Africa, she thought, and she couldn't stop herself from going, just as Deval couldn't stop himself, or his men, from killing and being killed. She wrapped her arms around herself again.

'Why this sudden desire to fight for the glory of France?' she asked.

'It is simply a matter of expediency,' he explained. 'I am ambitious. I am also impatient. As the situation is at present, I will be fortunate if I make a full Colonel before I am due for retirement. That is not good enough, so I need something and somebody.' He looked pointedly at her, 'to help me on my way. In other words, I need some good publicity. Some public recognition.' He shrugged. 'The Legion is the only force to see any action. It has produced many Marshals of France. They all started by proving themselves in action.'

'And you intend to do the same?'

'The opportunities are limited, so if there is any action I want to be part of it.'

'And if you are killed in the challenge?'

'Then God will have won and I will have lost,' he laughed, 'but I do not think my destiny is to rot away in some barren desert in Africa.' He shook his head. 'I do not see that happening,' he said with conviction. He turned to face her.

'And why are you prepared to fly to Djibouti?' he asked.

'I am a journalist,' she replied, not looking at him. 'As you have already said – there is bush warfare going on in the territory. There could be a story in it. Your father thinks there is. He has asked me to go.'

'You could have refused.'

'He pays my salary cheque.'

'You could still have refused,' he said. 'Why did you really come here? Because of me, or because of yourself? Or because of them?' He pointed with his arm to the fortress.

She didn't answer him. She lit a cigarette instead.

'We are two of a kind, Jaquie,' he said. 'We come from the same stables. We can have anything money can buy, so instead we look for something money can't buy. I want to make a name for myself and I want to make it quickly. Africa might be able to help me. As for you...' He looked hard at her. 'I'll tell you why you are here, Jaquie. It's not because I asked you to come, or because my father asked you to go to Djibouti. You came because you were bored. Bored with your weekly press column. Bored with your parties and your empty love affairs. You were bored with life. The Legion and Africa interests you. They offer you something else to think about. That is why you are here and that is why you will be in Djibouti.'

He sat back. She didn't say anything. She knew that he was right. Like him, she had been looking for kicks – for some escape from her routine, but there was a little more to it than what he had said. She wasn't quite so disenchanted with life, or people, as Deval appeared to believe. She was concerned about people, and now she was very concerned about Deval and the men who would come under his command. She knew that their destiny was tied to Deval's – and to her own.

'I hope your men don't disappoint you,' she said.

'Or you,' he added, raising his glass in a gesture. 'Perhaps I might be able to arrange for you to talk to them – or rather one of them. It might add a bit of spice for you. We will see. Shall we go and dine now?'

FIVE

'Debout! – Debout!'

It was four a.m. again. Another day was about to begin. Again Cato moved quickly. It was their last day of training in Bonifacio, but Cato and the other men selected for posting were now under Sergeant Bouchier. He was making their lives a hell. He would surpass himself on their last day. Cato steeled himself. But suddenly before the battle between the men and Bouchier began, Cato found an unexpected oasis. He was allowed a short break from the routine – an unbelievable short breath of freedom.

At the morning parade, he was detailed to report to Lieutenant Deval. The order took him by surprise. He had never spoken to the Lieutenant, or any other officer. He was marched to Deval's quarters by a Corporal. The Corporal was dismissed and Cato ordered into the room. He entered the room and stood stiffly to attention. He felt Deval's eyes studying him, critically.

'Stand at ease, legionnaire,' Deval ordered.

Cato stood at ease. He could see Deval from the corner of his eye. He was dressed in his field uniform ready for the range. He was a smaller man than Cato had thought – smaller and slimmer.

'You are an American, I understand,' Deval said.

'Yes, *mon Lieutenant*,' Cato replied, and wondered if that had anything to do with him being in Deval's room.

'My orderly is not available today,' Deval said watching Cato intently. 'I would like you to undertake his duties.'

Orderly to Deval! The thought rankled Cato. He had never been servant to any man. He didn't take to such duties. He made no comment, but Deval must have suspected his feelings.

'There are certain privileges, legionnaire,' Deval said, as if offering a titbit to an animal. 'For instance, I would like you to take my uniform to the tailor in the town, and deliver a letter to a friend.'

There was an immediate smell of freedom in Deval's remarks. Suddenly a window had been forced open and a breath of fresh air had been blown into the room. Cato was being offered the opportunity to walk through the town. For almost four months he had never been given one minute to himself, other than the periods in his sleep. Now he was being offered the opportunity to walk about like a free man.

'You will tidy my room and clean my equipment,' Deval said. He knew that Cato could not refuse his bait. 'That is all that is required.'

He went to a cupboard. He returned holding a uniform. For a moment their eyes met and Cato looked into Deval's vague, hazel eyes. He saw that they were mocking him. There was a look that said, 'You poor sod. I knew that you couldn't refuse the thought of freedom'.

'This is the uniform,' Deval said. 'The guard room will give you your pass. Here is the letter. I would like you to take it to Mademoiselle Chauvier. She is staying at the Hotel by the harbour. You are to give it to her personally. She is a journalist. She might ask you questions. You are free to talk to her.' He laid the envelope on the table.

'You will report back to the guard room at 0930 precisely. You will then be taken to the range.' A faint smile appeared on his face. 'I don't think you will try to desert – yet.'

Cato looked at him with surprise. It was not a remark that he had expected from an officer.

'I have no such intention, *mon Lieutenant*,' he said.

'Perhaps not at present,' Deval agreed, 'but you will in time. It is not unusual in the Legion.'

He gave a faint smile of amusement, and walked past Cato and left the room.

Cato frowned. He didn't like Deval's sense

61

of humour or the way he thought he knew what was in Cato's mind. It was as if Deval knew more about him than he knew himself.

He set about his tasks and soon forgot about Deval. When he had finished his duties, he reported to the guard *poste*. His rifle was taken from him and he was given a pass to permit him into the town. He left the guard *poste* and walked through the gates, and past the *sentinelle*. For a moment he stood in the open, breathing in his freedom. It was early morning with the scent of freshness in the air. There was no one about. It was too early for the tourists to come and stare at the sentry. He crossed over to a parapet wall and looked down at the harbour. Far below him was the U-shaped harbour inlet with its calm dark, grey water. Along the sides of the harbour were the boats that had come from all parts of the Mediterranean. They were part of the holiday scene, just as the rows of red and blue umbrellas outside the harbour cafes were also part of the holiday scene. That was the tourist part of the city, he thought. That was another world.

He walked down the road that led from the fortress city to the harbour. He had covered the ground regularly, but always under the eagle eyes of the N.C.O.'s – always on the alert – always part of the drilled machine.

On that particular morning he walked slowly, enjoying every minute of his freedom. He left the uniform with the tailor and walked around the harbour. The waiters at the cafes were washing down their pavements and preparing their tables for the breakfasts. He stood and admired the boats. They reminded him of a time that he had spent on a boat similar to those in the harbour. It had been the time he had met his wife. It had been a long time ago.

He went to the hotel. It was close to the harbour on the road that led out of the town. He entered its foyer and felt strange in its lush atmosphere. The hotel staff were preparing the reception area for the early risers. They eyed him with curiosity. He went to the reception counter. A young man looked at him enquiringly.

'I wish to see Mademoiselle Chauvier,' Cato said.

'It is early,' the receptionist replied, 'but I will see if she is available.'

He rang a room number. Cato stood back and glanced at the marble, mosaic floor and coloured ornaments that decorated the room.

'Room number 401, Monsieur,' the receptionist said. 'Mademoiselle Chauvier is expecting you.'

Cato took the lift to the fourth floor and found room 401. He knocked on the door.

There was a moment's delay, then the door opened, and Jaquie Chauvier stood in front of him.

Cato didn't say anything. He stood looking at her as if he was taken aback by what he saw. She was slim, petite and evenly tanned. Her hair was fair and long, and her eyes brown, but it was her smile that held his attention. It was broad and friendly and seemed to light up her whole face. She was wearing a pale blue, summer dress with a matching piece of ribbon in her hair. The shade of blue was delicate and feminine, and so was she. She had suddenly made him aware how basic and grey his life had become, and how much he missed the gentleness and femininity of his wife.

He continued to stare.

'Lieutenant Deval sent you?' she asked, in a softly spoken voice.

Cato got over his surprise. He looked slightly uncomfortable. He knew that he had been staring.

'Yes, Mademoiselle. I have a letter for Mademoiselle Chauvier.'

'I am Mademoiselle Chauvier.'

He fumbled in his pocket for the letter.

'Do come in, Monsieur... What is your name?'

'Cato, Mademoiselle – Lee Cato.'

She opened the door invitingly. Cato held the letter in his hand, and hesitated.

She smiled at him. She was being friendly. 'My name is Jaquie,' she said. 'I am just about to have some coffee. Please join me.'

She accepted the letter. Cato took off his white *képi* and entered the room.

'Excuse the mess,' she said. 'We will have coffee on the balcony.'

He followed her through the bedroom. It was a small room and seemed to have too much furniture. The balcony was even smaller, but it had a magnificent view of the harbour with the fortress high in the background.

'It does look magnificent,' she said, looking at the fortress.

'From here,' he agreed, and looked away.

'I can see you marching to the range,' she said.

'There are many tourists watching,' he replied.

'Do they annoy you?'

He shrugged.

She offered him a seat. He sat down at a table.

'I have ordered coffee and rolls. Is that suitable?'

'We normally don't eat until about ten o'clock.'

'Then this will be an extra meal today.'

She smiled at him again. He liked her smile. It wasn't patronising. It was warm, alive and friendly. It was like his wife's smile had been.

'You haven't told me about the tourists,' she said.

'I envy them,' he replied, and dropped his eyes.

'Why?' she asked.

Why? he wondered. Was it their freedom or their happiness? Or was it their peace of mind? It was their peace of mind, he thought. Above all else it was their peace of mind and their happiness.

He shuffled in his seat.

'You are visiting Bonifacio?' he asked, changing the subject.

She understood and didn't take offence. She liked the look of him. He looked fresh and clean cut. She liked his strong, tanned features, his clear, blue eyes, and the way his chin looked firm and proud. He looked like a man who knew what he wanted and went after it.

'I am a journalist from Paris,' she said. 'I work for Lieutenant Deval's father. He owns several newspapers. I am on my way to Djibouti.'

'Djibouti?' Cato asked.

'Why are you surprised?'

He shrugged. 'That is where I am to be sent, also,' he said.

'We have a newsagency syndicate in Djibouti,' she explained. 'I am going to work there for several weeks.'

'You will find it very different from Paris.'

'Very,' she agreed, 'and much hotter, but at present it is in the news quite often, so there might be something interesting for me to write about. Do you know anything about the territory of Afars and Issas?'

'Just that it used to be called French Somaliland,' he said. 'It is very hot and very barren, and the tribespeople regularly fall out with each other.'

'It is also a very busy port in East Africa and with all the trouble in the Middle East, I suppose it is now very important to France.'

'Important to France,' Cato commented.

'You do not agree?' she asked.

It was his turn to smile.

'It is not my place to say what is important to France,' he said.

'Very diplomatic,' she said.

A waiter brought the breakfast tray to the balcony. Cato glanced at his watch.

'Do you have a time limit?' she asked.

'Yes. Like Cinderella I must return to my duties at a certain time.'

'Soon?'

'Yes.'

'That is a pity.'

He looked up at her. Their eyes met and he knew she had meant what she said. He wondered why she was being so nice to him.

'Yes, it is,' he agreed and looked away.

'You are an American?' she asked in English.

'Is my accent so bad?' he asked.

She laughed. 'No. You speak it well, but I could tell.'

'Have you ever been to the States?' he asked.

She continued to speak in English.

'Yes, several times. It was part of my studies. Where did you live?'

He frowned. She saw it.

'Sorry,' she said. 'I was beginning to pry. I should have known better. One never asks a legionnaire about his past. I am sorry.'

'I lived in Norristown, near Philadelphia,' he said, 'but I would rather not talk about it.'

'I understand.'

Again he felt that she did understand. There was something about her that was genuine. He drank his coffee.

'Lieutenant Deval said that you might wish to question me about the Legion,' he said.

'But you would rather not talk about it?' she asked.

He looked up at her. She smiled again.

'No,' he agreed, and smiled back at her.

'All right,' she said. 'I will not ask about it then. We will just talk and enjoy our coffee and the fresh morning air.' She picked up a packet of cigarettes and offered him one. He refused. She lit her cigarette.

'You are the Lieutenant's orderly?'

'Only for today. His orderly is sick.'

She raised her eyebrows as if questioning the statement.

'Are there any other Americans in the camp?' she asked.

'There is one other,' he replied. 'I do not know him very well.'

'And will you soon be leaving for Djibouti?'

'Yes, very soon. Tomorrow we march to Corte.'

'To Corte! That is a long way.'

'The march signifies the end of our training,' he explained.

'Are you pleased?'

'Yes,' he said. 'I am looking forward to Djibouti.'

'So am I,' she smiled.

He finished his coffee and saw that it was time to leave. He frowned. She saw it.

'You have to leave?' she asked.

'Unfortunately,' he replied. He liked talking to her. She was so relaxed. It was like being with an old friend.

He stood up.

'If you will excuse me, Mademoiselle,' he said.

She also stood up.

'Perhaps we can continue our conversation in Djibouti,' she suggested.

He looked uncertain.

'But the Lieutenant...'

'He is a friend,' she said. 'I can see who I wish.'

'I see.'

'I will be staying at the Hotel Imperial. Will you call on me?'

'I would like to.'

She held out a hand.

'Then I will expect you,' she said. 'You won't forget.'

He took her hand. It felt very soft. It made him feel unsure of himself, but he didn't want to let go. He wanted to hold on to it. She gave him a smile. He let go of her hand, apologetically.

'*Au revoir*,' she said. 'I will be expecting you.'

'*Au revoir*,' he mumbled and left her.

He walked away from the hotel in a semi daze. He didn't know whether she was watching him from her balcony or not, and he didn't turn to see. She had reminded him of a lot that he had forgotten, but it was all with him again, and so was the pain. He increased his pace and tried to forget about the girl, but she had left an impression on him that was difficult to erase.

Jaquie Chauvier was watching him from her balcony. She watched him until he disappeared out of her sight, and then stared long and hard at the Citadel. She had also been left with an impression that she knew was going to be difficult to erase. She had been very attracted to Cato.

That night as Cato lay on his bunk, he thought about Jaquie Chauvier. He wondered why she was in Bonifacio, and why Deval had selected him to confront her. He could only deduce that they knew about his past and that he was a curiosity to them. It irritated him to think that they had put him under their microscope. He fell asleep thinking about her. When he awoke she was forgotten. It was another day – the day they marched as legionnaires were expected to march. It was their last test of endurance as trainees.

They left the fortress in the early hours of the morning, wearing full battle equipment, on a non-stop route march across the Corsican mountains to the town of Cortes in the heart of the island. Accompanying them was a convoy of trucks, with their ration and field kitchens, and a helicopter that hovered overhead in case any of them attempted to desert. The helicopter was unnecessary. The march was too gruelling for anyone to even think of desertion.

Their feet ached and bled, but still they marched, or were dragged along by the vehicles like animals. Sergeant Bouchier and Corporal Schnell marched with them.

71

Bouchier seemed to be enjoying the opportunity to show off his physical fitness. He matched the men in equipment and faced the same physical challenge. Any sign of slackness by the men brought his cane into instant action.

Vasey survived the ordeal with the least effect. His delight showed on his face and his chest seemed to swell in pride. The others all felt the physical exhaustion of the march and some like Sasous and Fritz needed medical attention, when they arrived at their destination. They were taken into the sick bay.

The Citadel at Corte was old, basic and depressing, but the men welcomed it as the end of the march.

Bouchier's group of men were barracked together to await their posting. They were a strange collection of men – a mixed group of nationals each with their own particular problems, attitudes and ways, but they had trained together during their last week at Bonifacio and they were to serve together. They accepted each others peculiarities and each other. There was no other way in the Legion.

Cato visited Sasous in hospital soon after his admission and learned that even in hospital Sasous had started his enquiries about the two men that Cato wanted to know about.

'There is a clerk in the records office,'

Sasous said with a knowing smile. 'I have arranged for him to be approached. He will give us the information.'

But the information was not forthcoming. Later in the week when Cato visited Sasous again, nothing had been heard from Sasous' contact. Cato was concerned. He had to get to know the whereabouts of the two men when he was in Corte, and he would soon be moving out. He knew that under normal circumstances the details of a legionnaire's posting would be available, but if there was any suspicions of the motive of the enquiry, there would be a stubborn refusal to give any information. The Legion protected its own and legionnaires, in particular, protected each other.

'We must be cautious,' Sasous warned, voicing Cato's concern. 'They know the information if for you. That has aroused their curiosity. They must be suspicious.'

'I could request it officially,' Cato said.

'You could, but that would not be prudent. They would want to know why you want the information, and the word would soon be passed to the two men in question. It would be wise to be cautious. Besides, I will be returning to duties in two days. I will visit this clerk myself. Do not worry, *mon ami*. I will get the information for you. Perhaps a little more money will get results.'

As events turned out, Cato got the information the following day, but in a manner, and for a reason, that he had not anticipated. It was the day of the tests. The day that the men were officially put through their tests by a team of officers and N.C.O.'s.

One by one, Cato and the men of the Section were questioned and tested. All but Vasey, passed with ease. Vasey had to be helped like a small child who had to be led by the hand. Bouchier couldn't control his contempt and he excelled himself with his abuse and derision. Any delight that Vasey had felt at being physically equal to Bouchier on the march was soon forgotten.

When it was all over, Vasey was left smarting and smouldering under a cloud of despair. In the mess hall he was sullen and quiet. Afterwards he went to the canteen to drown his sorrows.

Cato returned to the barrack room and started preparing his equipment for the following day. So did some of the other men from their section.

Napoleon came into the room.

'There's going to be trouble in the canteen,' he told them all. 'They are riding Vasey again.'

Cato froze in the act of putting his equipment in his locker.

'The big Swede?' he asked.

'Yeah, Cato, the big Swede and his friends.'

Cato knew the group. They had kept

together at Bonifacio, and acted like a gang of mobsters. He finished tidying his locker. He had no love for Vasey. He had not even spoken to him since they had been thrown together, but he had felt for Vasey when he had been ridiculed by Bouchier and he felt for him now. Vasey would be on his own. He had teamed up with Irish but Irish was on *sentinelle*. Vasey would be on his own and the big Swede and his friends would be having their fun with him.

Cato gave a grunt and picked up his hat. All the frustration that had built up inside him at not getting the information about Mandril and Pescod, seemed to be wanting to get out of his system like an escape of steam. He wanted action and he wanted action against Pedrides and his kind, and the big Swede reminded him of Pedrides.

'Where are you going, Cato?' Diago asked. He had been lying on his bunk meticulously cleaning his knife.

'Canteen,' Cato said.

He didn't wait for any further discussion. He left the barrack room and went direct to the canteen. Diago went with him. Napoleon followed behind.

The canteen was large and noisy. The Citadel was the main training centre for recruits, but it as also used as a transit and posting camp. There were many veteran legionnaires in the canteen as well as trainees.

'Beer?' Diago asked.

Cato didn't hear him. He had seen Vasey sitting at the end of a table by himself. He looked like an animal being baited. At the next table was the big, blond Swede and his group of toughs. It wasn't difficult to gather what was going on. They were goading Vasey, and Vasey couldn't bring himself to get up and leave them. He wanted to fight them, but he had enough sense to know that the Swede and his group fought like a pack of wolves. They would tear him to pieces.

Cato went directly to his table. A hush seemed to settle around the area.

'Another stupid American,' a voice called out from the Swede's table. It was followed by a roar of laughter.

'What's the matter, Vasey,' Cato hissed. 'Don't you like the odds?'

Vasey didn't look at him. He smouldered.

'I'm frightened of no one,' he growled.

'Good. The big Swede's mine. Just remember that.'

Cato stood up. His eyes were fixed on the big Swede and his mind had only one purpose. He went up to the big Swede. All his resentments and frustrations went with him.

'I don't think Americans are stupid,' he shouted. 'I think you are stupid. You are a stupid *cochon.*'

The Swede gave a roar and got to his feet. Cato hit him instantly. His fist crashed into

76

the Swede's face and sent him sprawling. The Swede got to his feet and came at Cato. Again Cato hit him, and suddenly all hell seemed to be let loose. Something hit Cato on the side of his head, but he was only vaguely aware of it. He went at the big Swede with his fists flying. He lashed into him and he fought with all the tricks the Legion had taught him. He fought dirty, but that was the way of the Legion. The Legion was a jungle and it was a jungle fight. He was only half conscious of the mêlée that was going on around him.

Suddenly he felt his arms being pinned together behind his back.

'Enough!' a voice ordered. 'Enough!'

He struggled to free himself, but his arms were held tight.

'Enough!'

Cato was swung round. It was Corporal Schnell who held him.

'Enough, Cato,' he ordered. 'You have proved your point.'

Cato calmed down. He saw the big Swede sprawled on the floor. There were two others beside him. He breathed easier. Schnell let him go. He turned and saw Vasey. He was all bloody and his shirt was torn, but he had a smile on his ugly face. But it wasn't only Vasey and Cato who had been in the fight. Diago had also joined in. He was also bruised and bleeding.

'Get cleaned up, Vasey,' Schnell ordered.

Cato looked at Diago and asked, 'Why?'

Diago shrugged his shoulders.

'It seemed a good idea at the time,' he said. 'I'll get some beer.'

Cato went to an empty table to lick his wounds. His knuckles were bleeding and his face was cut and bruised.

A figure appeared in front of him. It was a legionnaire with a row of campaign ribbons. Cato had never spoken to him before, but he recognised him as a member of the permanent staff. The man slid a bottle of beer across the table. Cato took a drink.

'A mutual friend told me that you are interested in two packages,' the man said.

Cato's pulse quickened. He knew that the two packages that the man was referring to were Mandril and Pescod. The two men that he was looking for!

'Very interested,' he said.

'They were delivered to an infantry regiment in the 13th,' the man said, and stood up and left the table before Cato could thank him.

Cato said a mental prayer of thanks and gave a grunt of satisfaction. The 13th was the 13th Demi-Brigade with its headquarters in Djibouti. It was the brigade that Cato was also being sent to. The two men were not going to be in Cato's unit, but they were in the same territory. It was all beginning to take shape. He was getting near his goal. Diago joined him with the beer.

'Some night,' he said.

'It sure is,' Cato agreed, but he was very glad that he had come to the canteen and fought it out with the Swede. If he hadn't he might not have learned about Mandril and Pescod. There was a strange code of honour amongst the men of the Legion. There had to be respect. Cato had earned that respect by standing up to the Swede.

Vasey returned to the canteen. He had cleaned himself and changed his shirt. He came to their table. He looked hesitant.

'Thanks,' he mumbled.

'Sit down and have some beer,' Cato called out. 'Tonight we are going to celebrate.'

Vasey joined them. So did Corporal Schnell and Hessler. They all celebrated.

The following day Sasous and Fritz rejoined the group. Sasous looked at Cato's battered face and shook his head sadly.

'You Americans are so impulsive,' he sighed. 'Such a shame.'

'There was something I had to get out of my system,' Cato said.

'Don't let Bouchier hear you say that,' Sasous warned, 'or he'll have us all on extra duties.'

'I got the necessary information,' Cato said.

'I know,' Sasous smiled. 'That is good,

because we are leaving very soon, and we can use the money for other means.'

'Leaving soon?' Cato asked. 'When?'

'The day after tomorrow.'

Cato gave a broad smile, but didn't question Sasous' information.

SIX

On the day that Sasous had predicted, Cato and the other men of the section were flown to Djibouti, the capital of the French Territory of Afars and Issas. They landed at Djibouti Airport at mid-day and immediately felt the intense heat that made Djibouti one of the hottest ports in the world. They also caught its particular scent. The combination of camel dung and diesel fuel roasted under a baking sun was only part of the aromatic scents that greeted them.

The Garrison Camp was a collection of spartan, single storey, concrete block and timber buildings. It had an atmosphere of disciplined efficiency and few comforts. There was the intense heat, the desert scrub of the terrain, and the anticipation of combat that hung heavily in the air. Cato sensed it and so did the other men. Their training days were over. But Cato also sensed Mandril and Pescod and he soon found out that they were not in the garrison camp.

The men from Corte were kept together as replacements for a section which had suffered heavy losses in a skirmish with a terrorist band along the border with

Ethiopia. It was commanded by Captain Kubik, an ex-Polish Legionnaire, who had worked his way up from the ranks. He was a middle-aged man, with a reputation for firmness and discipline. Lieutenant Deval and Sergeant Bouchier came under his command. Bouchier and the Captain knew each other. The Captain greeted him civilly, but not warmly. The other Section Sergeant was a Hungarian called Trocco. He was a tall, wild-looking man, who had once been reduced to the ranks for fighting with his fellow N.C.O.'s in the mess, but he was a good soldier with several decorations for bravery and he had been promoted again. He was junior to Bouchier in rank and age, but he had served two years in the territory and was more experienced in the terrain and its warfare.

The men were barracked with the other members of the Section. When they arrived they were looked upon with a certain amount of caution that always greets strangers to a Unit, but in the mess hall and canteen the barriers were lowered, and questions were asked. What about Bouchier? Was he as tough as was said? Why had he come? Why had he left Corsica? And who was the Lieutenant?

It was not surprising that Sasous was one of the first to make contact with the other legionnaires. Two of them came up to him in the canteen. One was a dark man of medium height with a scar across his face and deep brown penetrating eyes. The other was tall, fair haired, with a friendly face and a ready smile. The two men seemed to be opposites in all things, except age. They were both slightly older than the rest of the Section. The smaller man's name was Raphael and he was a Frenchman from Dijon. Later they learned that he was also called *La Bohemien – The Gypsy*, because of his powers of clairvoyance and the forecasts that he had made over the past months. It was said that he had foreseen the death of some of the men in the Section who had later been killed in the fighting, and that he forecast a bloody battle that had yet to take place. The men of the Section treated him with great respect and were always keen to know what the Gypsy had *seen*. At their first meeting, Sasous and Cato were unaware of his uncanny gift. Raphael knew of Sasous by reputation and had come to pay his respects. He introduced his friend as Larse, a Norwegian from Lillehammer. Sasous introduced them to Cato and Greco, who were with him, and invited them to join their group. They sat down. Raphael produced a bottle of cheap brandy and Larse some cigarettes.

'An American?' Raphael asked Cato. 'Two in one Section. That is unusual.'

'Are there any other Americans in the

Brigade?' Sasous asked.

'No,' Raphael replied.

Sasous didn't pursue the line. Neither did Cato. They both knew that Pedrides would have changed his nationality just as he would have changed his name. They did not mention Mandril and Pescod by name either. It was wiser to let Sasous find out in his own time.

'Tell us what it is like here,' Greco said.

'The Captain is all right,' Larse explained. 'He is strict, but he knows his job. You have to watch the Sergeant. He has a quick temper and likes to mix it. With Bouchier supporting him they will be a couple of bastards to deal with. The Corporals are fair. They do not bully us like they did in Corsica, but the discipline is just as strict.'

'What happened to the others?' Sasous asked. 'The ones that didn't return?'

Larse looked at the Frenchman.

'In the hills it is barren and lonely,' Raphael said, and shrugged. 'One can easily think that there is nothing happening and suddenly they will be upon you.'

'Who?' Cato asked. 'There has been very little publicity about the fighting.'

Raphael shook his head.

'They do that on purpose,' he said. 'They want to keep it very local – very much in the background. If the word got around that there was trouble it might attract all the other tribes, and they don't want any interference from any outsiders.'

'Who does all the fighting?' Greco asked. 'Are they well organised?'

'They come and go,' the Frenchman scowled. 'They are led by a man called Hakim. We call him the Mad Mullah. They occasionally blow up the railway line that runs to Ethiopia and sometimes they attack the *postes*. They say that there is only about a hundred of them. They also say that they are encouraged by holy men, but,' the Frenchman became secretive, 'we have heard that they are being supplied and equipped by the Communists. They are just stirring up trouble. They want the French out of the country.'

'What about the Air Force? Can't they get them?' Sasous asked.

The Frenchman shook his head.

'They hide where they cannot be seen from the air,' he said. 'We go out to the *postes* and stay there for several weeks, and do reconnaissance patrols. We then come back to the camp and do everything from road mending to general duties.' He shrugged. 'The other Sections have also lost many men.'

'And where are these *postes*?' Cato asked.

'They are on the borders close to the mountains. They are very isolated. There is little comfort.'

He poured the brandy into the glasses

again. The men took a drink. Irish, Napoleon and Vasey came over to join them.

'What's in the town?' Irish asked.

'Everything you can wish for,' Raphael explained. 'They call the big place Rosie's.' There was a gleam in his eyes. 'They tell me that it is as good as it was in Sidi Bel Abbes when the Legion was in Algeria.'

'Perhaps that is why Bouchier wanted to come back,' Irish suggested.

'To hell with Bouchier,' Napoleon said. 'Where is this joint?'

Raphael told him, and he answered all his questions about the delights in store for them at Rosie's. But it was some time before the men were given leave. First they had to be drilled and trained to suit their new terrain. They were immediately introduced into a regular, and rigorous routine of training and camp duties. The only difference from their routine in Corsica was at mid-day when even the Legion had to succumb to the intense heat of the sun. For three hours the men rested and sweated. Some suffered the heat better than others. Men like Sasous, Greco, Diago, Hessler and Fritz would lie on their bunks with their thoughts far away. Others like Hook, Boussec and Irish sweated and cursed. Hook was sharp tempered and belligerent. Cato also suffered. He had never known such heat, but gradually, like the rest, he got used to it.

Bouchier and Sergeant Trocco kept the men at it and gave no quarter. They gave out punishment for the slightest offence and the men hated their guts.

Lieutenant Deval watched over them from a distance. He came and went like a mirage and prompted Greco to remark, dryly, one day, 'Regardez – *Monsieur Le Pimpernel.*' Unfortunately, he had spoken too loud and Bouchier overheard him. As a result, Greco spent an hour that evening undergoing corrective discipline for insubordination, but the title he had given Deval had been appropriate. Deval did come and go like the Pimpernel, and the title would have stuck had the men come into contact with him more often, or if they had cause to refer to him. As it was, he kept his distance and gave all his orders through Sergeant Bouchier. Later when the men did become more directly involved with him, he earned himself another less complimentary title.

Sasous soon set about making his contacts and cultivating his grapevine. It was second nature to him and his eyes would light up with delight whenever he told Cato about a new contact, or learned some special piece of information. He was like an artist being given the opportunity to show off his skills and talents. At other times, however, he could have a sad, far away, look in his eyes and Cato would know that he was back in Paris.

Sasous made contact with the camp quartermaster – a large, burly Portuguese who had lived in Paris before joining the Legion and whose path had crossed over similar ground as Sasous. From him, Sasous acquired extra luxuries and also an introduction to the Corporal Clerk in the Adjutant's office. It was not long before he was able to tell Cato that Mandril and Pescod were both stationed at one of the Legion's border *postes*.

Cato greeted the news of the whereabouts of the two men calmly, although he knew that it was just a question of time before he caught up with them. But when Sasous gave him the news, he also put a question to him that had never been bought into the open before.

'What will you do when you find your man?' he asked.

Cato thought before replying. His cause had been to find the man – to prove that he existed. It had driven him on blindly. It had kept him going. Now he had to think beyond that. He had to think what he was going to do when he found Pedrides.

'I would like to kill him,' he said.

'And yourself also?' Sasous asked. He shook his head, sadly. 'I do not think you are a murderer, *mon ami,* and the Legion's punishment battalions are very severe.'

Cato shrugged. His inside always turned

cold at the very thought of Pedrides.

'The Legion will not want to know about him,' he grumbled, 'but he has to be punished.'

'At the right time and in the right manner,' Sasous said.

'The time and manner might never be right,' Cato sighed.

'Perhaps,' Sasous shrugged. 'We will see. Come, let us go to the canteen. We will worry about your revenge when the time comes.'

The following morning, Bouchier gave Cato and the men something else to think about. They were paraded in full combat equipment, but still wearing their *képi-blancs*, their traditional white hats and neck flaps. When they assembled they saw a look on Bouchier's face that told them that it was not to be a normal day's training.

After the ceremonial parade of hoisting the *'Tri-colore'* had been performed, Bouchier turned on the men.

'You are going to see some of the countryside,' he shouted. 'I am going to show you what you might die for!'

He marched them out of the camp and on to the desert plain that they had only caught glimpses of during their training runs. Captain Kubik and Lieutenant Deval went with them, but the two officers went with the vehicles. It was left to the Sergeants to drill, discipline and cajole the men, and Bouchier revelled in it. He marched with them shouting out his orders in his rough, coarse accent, still wearing his gloves and carrying his cane, which he let loose at random. Sergeant Trocco was always alongside him and his tall, powerful frame and quick temper warned anyone against making any protest, physical or otherwise.

Cato and the men marched silently, conserving their energy. The sun was a large, yellow furnace over their heads. The first hour seemed endless, the second was hotter. Ahead of them appeared an endless plain of baked sand, prickly, wizened shrubs and bushes, and patches of yellow vegetation. All under the blazing sun and the *kharif*, the warm wind that was constantly drying the perspiration from their bodies and blowing the sand into their faces. Occasionally they got a glimpse of a Somali, or Afar, herdsman. They would suddenly appear – tall, detached, in a cotton robe that might have once been white. Across their shoulders was a rifle, or a stick, and at their feet trailed a scraggy herd of sheep or goats. They would come and go like a mirage, without appearing to notice the column of men. The men also got a glimpse of a native tribe on the move with their herds of cattle and camels, but they didn't interest themselves. They marched and perspired, and the

90

perspiration dried on their bodies.

At night they were still in the desert scrub. They mounted *sentinelles* around the camp and felt the cold of the night as the temperature dropped.

The night was a strange experience for them. The *kharif* turned into a cold breeze during the night, and the moonlit sky made the night almost as bright as daylight. The scrub and bushes cast shadows that moved with the breeze, and there were the mosquitos and the many other insects that all became active during the night. Hook voiced his grumbles about them until Bouchier ordered him to be quiet in his rough, barking voice that carried far across the plain. All noises were magnified at night. But for Cato there was something majestic and peaceful about the night, and he could think of the past without the burning pain.

The Section stayed three days on the plains. Three days of the *kharif.* Three days of the swirling sand that got into their eyes, their nostrils, and their ears. It found its way into everything. They felt the eerie isolation of the terrain and saw the wandering nomadic tribesmen who survived on a meagre existence and an unswerving faith in the will of Allah.

The men of the Section didn't come to know the plains of the desert, or the people, but they came to respect them and treat them with caution.

The return to their camp was like returning to a paradise. The spartan conditions of the barracks were like a palace. But their stay in the barracks was not to be a rest cure. They were kept busy. They exercised in further manoeuvres on the plain with their scout cars – small mobile vehicles armed with either a machine gun or a mortar, and with a crew of three personnel. In these vehicles they saw more of the desert.

Finally, Cato and the men from Corsica were given their first taste of freedom – a twelve hour pass. They left the camp in pairs and groups to explore the town and the delights of Rosie's. Diago and Fritz went together. Diago liked to talk about his native Spain, and Fritz was a good listener. Vasey went with Irish, and Hook and Boussec always kept together. Hessler joined Corporal Schnell and another group of Germans. Only Berge and Napoleon went alone. Berge went to seek out his own particular brand of company. Napoleon went straight to Rosie's. He wasn't interested in touring the town.

Greco joined Cato and Sasous. Sasous had a contact in the town that he wanted to visit. He was an exiled Parisian like himself. An ex-criminal who ran a bar near the docks.

As soon as Sasous entered the bar, he was welcomed like royalty. The ex-Parisian and his wife lavished attention on him, and also on Cato and Greco. Sasous was with his own kind and he revelled in their discussions of former days in Paris. Cato and Greco were content to take a seat in the wings. Later, Greco left them to visit Rosie's. Cato toured the town and found himself standing outside the imposing entrance of the Hotel Imperial. It was not by accident that he had gone there. He had often thought of Jaquie Chauvier and her invitation to visit her. He thought of her again as he stood and watched the European guests come and go. Finally, he turned his back on the hotel. He was unsure how genuine her invitation had been, and he had a feeling of guilt at wanting to see her again. He still hadn't come to terms with himself. He rejoined Sasous and joined in his celebration.

SEVEN

When Lieutenant Deval had joined the Garrison in Djibouti, he had immediately got the scent of action, like his men. He had, also, learned that there was trouble on the border and that the Legion would soon be called on to deal with it. When he had heard the news, he had felt the constrained excitement of a gambler who sensed that he was soon to be given his opportunity to play a hand in the big league. He knew that it was just a question of time before he would prove himself.

He had quickly settled into the life of the Unit in all its activities, both military and social. He knew that if he was to rise the ladder of success it wasn't only going to be because of his military achievements. He would also need the support and recommendations given in other quarters.

Captain Kubik, to whom Deval was attached, was a dedicated Legion Officer. He had accepted Deval without hesitation and went out of his way to teach him the art of warfare in the heat of their terrain. He also tried to instil in Deval a respect and interest for the men under his command and the natives who lived off the country. Deval was shrewd enough to appreciate what simple motives Kubik had in mind and was prepared to play along with him, but, in truth, he had little respect for his men, or the natives. But his men did interest him, especially the men that he brought with him from Corsica and who had now become his particular responsibility. He watched them from afar, but nevertheless he watched them, and, like Sasous, he had his own way of getting information about them. He knew that Diago and Greco still kept their distance; that Hook and Boussec behaved like animals, and that Bouchier was still riding Vasey. He knew that Hessler never closed his eyes at night and was modelling himself on Corporal Schnell; that Irish still called out in his sleep, and that Fritz was still full of an inner hatred of himself. He knew that Greco had been disciplined for referring to him as *Monsieur Le Pimpernel,* and that Cato and Sasous were asking about two men stationed at the border *postes.* He knew a lot about his men and they did interest him – especially the enquiries of Cato and Sasous.

Outside the Garrison, the social life of Djibouti offered every opportunity for personal pleasures to a young, handsome Officer. All the doors were open to Deval and that included many bedroom doors if he so wished. But Deval held back from having an affair. He had his burning ambition to succeed. He also had no desire to feel the warmth of a naked woman lying alongside him. The thought used to make him perspire. That was why he liked having Jaquie around. She was sisterly; she was friendly. She never expected sex, or if she did, she never asked for it. Perhaps she understood him, he used to think. Perhaps there was more to their relationship than he realised. Whatever the cause, he was very glad she was in Djibouti. She was his escape – his excuse. She had acquired a flat in a small, modern block and it became a welcome retreat for him, but a short while after their arrival he began to see a change in her. She was working on the staff of the news agency. Her days were full. She became involved in the affairs of the city and the country. She occasionally visited Deval at the camp, but she seemed to have lost some of her youthful vitality and zest for enjoyment. It was as if she was waiting for something to happen. He noticed the change and mentioned it. She shrugged it off with a reference to the heat – the excuse that was offered in Djibouti for any physical or mental change, but, in truth, she was waiting for something to happen. She was waiting for the wheel of destiny to make another turn, as she knew it would.

'In North Africa it is *le cafard*,' Deval

96

smiled. 'Here it is always the heat.'

'What about you?' she asked. They were on the balcony of her apartment, when Deval had raised the subject. Ahead of them were the lights of the harbour and the silhouettes of the ships and buildings.

'There was a fresh outburst of trouble on the border,' he replied. 'We lost some men. Something will have to be done about it.'

She turned to face him.

'I think you will get your wish soon,' she sighed. 'The security forces believe that there has been a fresh supply of arms smuggled in. Although heaven knows why anybody should want to fight and die for this place.'

'The Somalis have always been warlike,' Deval replied. 'Perhaps it is also because of the heat.'

He poured himself a drink. 'Your news about the arms smuggling encourages me,' he said. 'We are due to move up to the border soon.'

'Do you really want to fight and kill so much?' Jaquie asked.

Deval smiled. 'I think I would rather fight the Mad Mullah and his band of men than some of the wives of the Government officials.'

Jaquie didn't pass comment. She sat staring out across the harbour. She wasn't thinking of Deval's problem, or the problem of the social world of the port. She was thinking of Cato and the look in his eyes when they had talked in Bonifacio. They had met and talked for only a very short while, but he was still there in the back of her mind. She had tried desperately to forget him; to put him out of her thoughts altogether. But she knew so much about him, that she felt as if she had known him for a long time, and she was attracted to him. Immediately they had met, she had been attracted. It was there and there was nothing she could do about it. No matter how she tried, she couldn't rid herself of him. She had become engrossed in every aspect of her assignment. She had wrapped herself in an energetic working and social life. But Cato was still there. His face, his blue eyes, his sudden look of surprise when he had encountered her, and his problem. She thought of him whenever she visited the camp, or saw a legionnaire in uniform in the town. She thought of him when Deval talked about his desire for action. She wanted to know how he felt about it and whether the heat and the desert were affecting him, and if his heart was still sad and filled with revenge. She wanted to know a lot about Cato, but she couldn't voice her thoughts to Deval. Just as Deval couldn't voice his personal fears to her. They both used each other for support and company, but they didn't really know each other.

EIGHT

Shortly after the men's leave, Lieutenant Deval was detailed to take a convoy of supplies to the most northerly *poste* on the border. He picked his men from the section. Cato and Sasous were amongst those selected. So were Berge and Fritz. The men welcomed the detail as a change from their routine. Cato welcomed it because of Pedrides. Neither he nor Sasous made any reference to his search for Pedrides, but they both knew that his moment of truth could be close. The two men that Sasous had uncovered – Mandril and Pescod – were on duty in one of the *postes*. They might not be at the particular *poste* that the convoy was visiting, and neither of them might turn out to be Pedrides, but this was the closest that Cato was going to get to his goal for some time. His inside told him so. His flashing eyes and tight lips also told Sasous. As they were loading the trucks, Sasous put his hand, gently, on Cato's arm.

'Use caution,' he urged.

Their eyes met. Sasous gave a friendly smile, and moved away. Cato clenched his fist. One of the two men had to be Pedrides, he said to himself. He just had to be.

The convoy consisted of Deval's small, military command vehicle, two scout cars, and three stores trucks. Cato was detailed to one of the stores trucks with Fritz and a legionnaire driver. They left the camp at dawn, and travelled west following a route close to the railway line that linked the port with Ethiopia. The wind was in their faces – hot, clammy, dusty. It got inside the vehicles and covered the men with a layer of yellow sand. At mid-day the heat was unbearable. The vehicles were like red hot ovens. They came to a watering point and rested in what little shade they could get from the vehicles.

In the afternoon, they veered north and travelled on a compass bearing. There was no marked track, they made their own as they went. The mountains were visible on the horizon – rising very high, and brown, with their peaks shimmering in the heat like a mirage.

A track gradually emerged and the terrain became less spartan. They saw small tribes on the move with their camels and herds of goats and sheep, and there was a hint that the wind was cooler. In the late afternoon they saw the *poste* in the distance. It stood at the foot of the mountain range – a small group of simple, white buildings that had a fort-like appearance in its layout and with the *Tri-colore* fluttering from a flagpole.

Behind it, the dark, vast range of mountains towered high into the sky.

Surrounding the *poste* was an encampment of native, beehive huts and a large area of dirty green vegetation. There was a cluster of palm trees that marked the precious water hole and herds of camels, sheep, and goats, grazing around the area. It all gave a welcome feeling of limited fertility after the harshness of the plain.

As the convoy drew closer to the station, the men could see the tall, dark skinned natives standing amidst their herds of camels and sheep, and a legionnaire on sentry duty at the entrance to the *poste*. Cato felt his inside turn over. He felt a tremor of excitement pass through his body that made him shake. This could be the day when he would come face to face with Pedrides. He clenched his fists and the perspiration rolled down his brow. Then suddenly his panic passed, and he felt a calmness again.

'I wonder what we guard out here that is so important?' Fritz called out.

'The pass,' the driver explained. He was a bronzed, Swiss legionnaire who had done the journey many times. 'This is one of the passes through the mountains into Ethiopia. There is another to the north where we have a small outpost. From the *poste* we run patrols along the border.'

'Why should anyone cross into Ethiopia?'

Fritz asked.

'Smuggling,' the Swiss replied.

'Smuggling what?'

The Swiss shrugged. 'Anything from dope to arms,' he said. 'Also slave traffic.'

'The *poste* looks as if it has been up for some time,' Cato remarked.

'That is so. It does not offer much comfort either, but compared with those poor bastards,' the Swiss moved his head indicating the tribespeople, 'it is a palace.'

The convoy drove through the ring of the tribal encampment. The dust from their vehicles swirled into the air and was blown by the wind, but the natives didn't move away. They stood silently watching the passing vehicles.

The convoy passed through the entrance to the station and came to a halt in the square. As the dust settled, the men saw that they were surrounded by the plain, white, concrete block buildings that barracked the men. The legionnaires of the *poste* came out of their quarters to greet them. They were bronzed, bearded men – some half naked. They came up to the vehicles and welcomed the men of the convoy with a friendliness and warmth that Cato had not come across before. It was as if they were greeting old friends.

Cato got out of his vehicle. Questions were hurled at him.

'How is Rosie's?'

'Any new girls there?'

'What is news from Djibouti?'

'How is...?'

And so it went on.

Sergeant Trocco gave orders to offload the stores. The men set to. Cato's eyes flashed about him – not at the almost primitive looking buildings of the *poste,* but at the faces of the men. None looked like Pedrides. They were all unfamiliar. Would Pedrides have grown a beard? he wondered. Would he have returned to his former appearance? Or would he have tried to change his appearance as much as possible? The questions passed through his mind as he offloaded the stores.

They finished their work and were detailed to one of the barrack blocks for the night. They took a shower and went to the mess hall. The men talked long and fast. Fritz and Cato sat together. Cato's eyes flashed about him. He searched all the faces looking for his man.

It was the same in the evening. There was plenty of *vino.* The legionnaires at the *poste* drank heavily and became loud and raucous. Some sang, others gambled. Cato and the other men from the convoy joined in, all except Fritz. He was not seen in the mess hall. He often preferred his own company in the evenings.

Later in the evening, a legionnaire came off guard duty. He sat by himself away from the other men. He was a slim, dark haired youth. Cato watched him suspiciously. The man had his back to him, but he could be the man he was looking for, he thought. He was about the right age – the same colouring – the same height and weight. The adrenalin flowed through Cato's body. His eyes became fixed on the man's back. The laughing, the singing, were forgotten. All that mattered was the man sitting brooding by himself. The man who could be Pedrides! Cato decided to find out. He stood up. Suddenly Sasous was with him.

'Come, *mon ami*,' he called out. 'Let us take some air.'

Cato hesitated, his eyes still fixed on the man sitting by himself.

'Come,' Sasous insisted. 'It is cool outside. The night air will be pleasant without the *kharif* swirling around us. Come!'

Cato held back. Sasous insisted.

'Come!' he ordered.

Reluctantly, Cato agreed. There had been an urgency in Sasous' voice that had got through to Cato. They left the mess hall. There was a full moon that made it almost daylight. There was no wind. They were protected by the walls of the barracks.

'Let us go to the perimeter,' Sasous suggested, and led Cato to the perimeter fence that surrounded the *poste*. It was a clear, starry night. They could see far across the plain.

'You get a grand view out here,' Sasous remarked.

'What gives?' Cato asked. 'You didn't drag me out to take the air.'

'I thought perhaps that you were going to speak to Bonnatti, and he doesn't like to be bothered.' Sasous gave a shrug. 'He is an orphan from Naples. He lives a lot in his past, like we all do, but the men all like him.'

'Bonnatti?' Cato asked. 'The dark eyed, slim...' He said no more. He understood. Sasous had prevented him from making a fool of himself.

They sat down, their backs to the barrack wall. It was cool and pleasant. They smoked a cigarette. Cato could feel the effects of the wine. It cushioned him against the hatred that had been inside him. It relaxed some of his anger – or was it that he was relieved that Bonnatti had not been the man he was looking for? Perhaps, he thought. He gave a half laugh.

'I was sure I would be able to recognise Pedrides,' he said. He picked up a handful of the yellow sand and let it trickle through his fingers. 'So sure,' he said, and shook his head, sadly.

'Perhaps neither of these men will be the one you are looking for. What then?'

'What then?' Cato asked. He shook his head. 'Then we start again,' he said. He turned to his friend and smiled. 'And you will have a greater challenge than before.'

'Ah! what a challenge,' Sasous said. 'It will be one I will enjoy.'

They stood up. Cato held his friend's arm. His face was serious.

'What about you?' he asked. 'Can I help you?'

Sasous' face clouded over and he simply said, 'No, *mon ami,* no.' Then he immediately brightened up. 'Come,' he said. 'We are getting too morbid and they are drinking all the *vino.* Let us go back before we are packed off to our beds.' He slapped Cato on the shoulders. 'Come.'

They rejoined the men in the mess hall. They were part of the unit again.

The next day the convoy was due to return to Djibouti, but at the dawn parade, Cato and Berge were ordered to remain with Lieutenant Deval. Sergeant Trocco was taking the convoy back to Djibouti, the Lieutenant had other plans.

The two men reported to the Lieutenant.

'I am visiting an outpost,' Deval told them. 'You will come with me.'

Cato explained to Sasous what was taking place. A look of concern passed over Sasous' face. Cato saw it.

'I wonder what the Lieutenant is up to?'

106

Sasous asked.

'Up to?' Cato asked. 'Why shouldn't he visit the outpost?'

Sasous shrugged. 'They are not part of his section. Still...' He brightened up. 'We will see you in Djibouti tomorrow, if not tonight.'

The convoy moved out. Deval's vehicle followed behind. Berge was driving and Cato sat in the rear. When the convoy headed east, Deval directed Berge to follow a track to the north, keeping close to the mountains.

The journey was slow and tortuous. The scenery of the mountains that towered over them soon lost their interest as the heat became unbearable. The hot breeze covered their faces with its yellow dust that parched their throats and irritated their nostrils. But Deval kept going. There was to be no relief until they reached their destination in the late morning.

The outpost was a small, tented encampment at the head of a deep valley that twisted its way into the mountain range. The camp was sited in a natural inlet in the side of the valley formed by a projecting spur, and looked out over the vast, flat plain. Alongside the encampment, was a large crater formed by a geological fault. It was filled with loose boulders and was referred to as the *hole*. It was from this natural *hole* in the ground that a well had been drilled and the precious water pumped up into a water tank.

In the foreground of the camp were three scout cars and four tents. Alongside the tents was a flagpole from which hung the *Tri-colore,* and a wooden look-out post. Behind the tents was a sandbagged entrance to a cave in the mountainside, which housed the supplies, and the sand-bagged bunker that protected the water tank.

The valley itself was wide and flat and covered with clumps of dirty green vegetation and sprinkled with petrified looking trees. Close to the camp was a *wadi* – a dried up river bed – that gave the suggestion that some day it would flow again with water. In the valley a handful of scraggy sheep attacked what little vegetation there was, but there was no sign of a native camp.

As Deval's vehicle approached the outpost, legionnaires came out of the tents and stood waiting to greet them. There was only a handful of them and, like the men at the *poste* they were all deeply bronzed and some were bearded.

Again Cato felt himself becoming tense. Again his eyes flashed around him as they drove into the area.

Deval stopped their car alongside the other vehicles. A bearded Sergeant reported to him and introduced himself as Sergeant Villier. The other men gathered around. Cato saw their tanned faces. They were lean, sharp, rough or bearded, but they weren't Pedrides.

'There is some refreshment in the tent,' the Sergeant said.

'I would like to go to the look-out,' Deval said. 'There is a tribe on the horizon.'

He went with the Sergeant. Berge and Cato were taken to a tent and given some food and drink. They talked to the men. Berge asked them about their duties. The men told him. It was lonely and hot, but they were left to themselves, and Sergeant Villier was all right.

'Strangely enough,' one of them said, 'Mandril prefers it out here. He even volunteers for it.'

Mandril! Cato's heart missed a beat. Mandril preferred it out there! He volunteered for it! Cato put down his cup. Suddenly it was all with him again.

'Where is he?' he asked.

'Up the side of the mountain,' someone replied. 'We have another look-out position there.'

'You O.K.?' Berge asked Cato.

'The heat,' Cato mumbled.

'It sure gets you,' someone agreed. 'Bloody heat and mosquitos.'

Cato left the tent. His inside was shaking like a leaf. He recalled the sudden look of concern on Sasous' face. Sasous knew that Mandril was at the *poste,* he thought.

'Legionnaire!'

Cato turned. It was Lieutenant Deval calling him. The Lieutenant was standing by the forward look-out post with the Sergeant. Cato reported to him.

'There is a tribe moving north across the horizon,' Deval said, studying his map. 'I want to know how many men there are – approximately. There is a look-out on the mountain side.' He hadn't looked at Cato as he had spoken.

Cato hesitated.

'*Mon Lieutenant.*'

Deval turned to him, but didn't look him in the eyes.

'Get on with it,' he snapped. 'Get to the post on the mountain side.'

Cato felt a dull ache in the pit of his stomach. Suddenly he knew that he was being brought face to face with the man that he wanted to kill, but he also knew that Deval was aware of it as well! In a flash, he knew that Deval knew all about him! That was why he had put him on stage in Bonifacio. That was why he had brought him to the outpost. He knew all about Cato and he knew all about Pedrides. He hadn't looked at Cato as he had given him his orders. He hadn't been able to! Now he had his back to him, but he had engineered the meeting! He was calling Cato's bluff!

The Sergeant spoke gruffly to Cato and pointed out the look-out position. Cato moved away – his legs moving mechanically and his eyes and mind blinkered. He stumbled up the mountain trail in a blind daze. His feet moved upwards. The perspiration, heat and physical exhaustion were forgotten. In his hands was his automatic rifle and his hands were clenched fiercely around the butt and the barrel. He tripped over some ankle deep scrub and fell to the ground, but he didn't feel any pain. He moved slowly upwards, but at the back of his mind was the thought that he was being propelled by Deval, like some clockwork soldier. He was Deval's toy.

The look-out post was on a projection that protruded from a ledge on the side of the mountain. It had a small, sandbagged wall and a canopy to protect the sentry from the sun. Cato came to the ledge and stood breathing heavily.

'Hullo!' Mandril called out. It wasn't a welcoming greeting. It was a call of acknowledgement. Cato saw him and felt his stomach turn over. Mandril was stripped to the waist and deeply tanned. He was small and slim. His face was clean shaven. On his head was his white hat. But he was the size and shape of Pedrides! Cato mentally ticked off the details given to him by the F.B.I. Pedrides was twenty-three years of age, five foot seven inches tall, and weighed 150 lbs. He was dark skinned, with grey eyes, jet black hair, and his own teeth. There were no known distinguishing marks or habits, except his beard.

Cato moved towards the post. Mandril came forward. He fitted the bill, Cato thought. He was the same size and weight as the man in the bank, and the face was Pedrides without the beard. It was just as the F.B.I. had shown him with their identity-kit drawings. He felt his inside go tight. He moved towards the man. He saw Mandril's eyes. They were grey, dull and cold – like the grey of a wet November day! He was Pedrides! Mandril was Pedrides! He felt himself start to shake.

'What brings you up here?' Mandril asked. His accent wasn't pure. It was foreign like Cato's.

Cato answered flatly, in English. 'The Lieutenant wants to know how many are in that tribe on the horizon.'

Mandril frowned. His face became sharp and grave. 'Speak in French,' he snapped. 'I don't understand English.'

'Don't you?' Cato asked, still in English. 'I was told that you speak it very well.'

Mandril understood. It was written on his face as his eyes became narrow and mean, and his thin lips were pressed tightly together.

'What's your game?' he snarled in French. His hands had found his rifle. He pointed it at Cato.

'I've told you,' Cato replied, still in English. 'I have to get the approximate numbers in that tribe.'

Mandril stood back with his rifle at the ready.

'Get on with what you have to do,' he hissed in French.

Cato held his own rifle. This was the moment that he had waited for. Standing before him was his wife's murderer – the man who had murdered his wife and son. Here was the man that he wanted to kill. Here was the man that he should kill!

'Get on with what you have to do,' Mandril said again.

Their eyes met.

'How many men in that tribe?' Cato snapped.

'There are the binoculars,' Mandril replied in English, with an American accent. He indicated a pair of binoculars on the sandbagged wall of his position.

'So you do speak English after all,' Cato said.

Mandril brought his rifle nozzle to point at Cato. 'What's your game?' he asked, menacingly, in English.

Cato looked at the nozzle facing him and at his own rifle pointing at Mandril. For a second time stood still. All it needed was for him to squeeze the trigger, he thought. One squeeze and he'd have avenged his family.

'Who are you?' Mandril hissed.

Cato heard him, but didn't reply. His fingers wouldn't squeeze the trigger! They were frozen rigid. They wouldn't squeeze it. It was as if his joints and reflexes had all seized up. He felt his stomach recoil and he wanted to throw up. He turned quickly away to control his feelings and felt a weakness pass through his limbs.

'There are thirty,' Mandril said in French. 'Tell the Lieutenant that they are armed.'

Cato turned away. His stomach was churning his guts. He moved quickly away from the post, along the ledge, and threw up. When he recovered, he turned to see Mandril watching him from the post, with his rifle still pointing at him.

'I will be back,' Cato hissed to himself. 'My God! I will be back.'

He retraced his steps. Like lead weights, he dragged his feet down the mountain side. Lieutenant Deval was waiting for him. This time he was looking into Cato's face, but it was Cato who couldn't return the look.

'Well?' Deval demanded.

'Thirty, *mon Lieutenant*,' Cato replied. 'They are armed.'

Deval grunted.

'That is the same size as the other two groups,' the Sergeant remarked. 'They are building up quite an army.'

Deval didn't reply to the Sergeant. Instead

114

he spoke to Cato.

'Are you all right, legionnaire?' he asked. 'You look as if you have seen a ghost.'

'I am all right, *mon Lieutenant*,' Cato replied, and knew that Deval was laughing at him.

'I wonder what has upset you?'

Cato hated Deval. From that moment he felt a hatred for the man almost as deep as he felt for the man in the look-out post. Deval had brought Cato to the outpost for the very purpose of testing him. He had put Cato to his test, and Cato had failed. Cato hated Deval and he hated himself.

'The sun, *mon Lieutenant*,' he said.

'Tell Legionnaire Berge that we are moving off,' Deval ordered, and turned his attention to the Sergeant.

The return to Djibouti was long and tedious. For Cato the physical discomfiture was not so hard to bear as the mental one. He had come face to face with Pedrides and done nothing about it. He was a failure and he hated himself, and he hated Deval for engineering the situation.

NINE

During the following days, Cato was morose and unapproachable. Sasous knew what was tormenting him. He had found out from Berge what had taken place at the outpost and he had known Mandril had been there. The rest he had deduced, but Cato didn't want to talk about it, so Sasous bided his time. Cato drank more *vino* than he had done previously and was quiet in company. He flung himself into the physical side of their work with extra vigour.

Eventually Sasous got Cato to open up. They were working alongside each other repairing a road. Cato was working with his usual grim determination.

'Why do you still punish yourself?' Sasous asked. 'You have done nothing wrong.'

Cato didn't look at him. For a moment Sasous thought that he wasn't going to respond, then Cato hissed, 'He was standing right in front of me. I could have killed him.'

He dug his spade into the ground with feeling.

'I walked away from him,' he added with disgust. 'I did nothing. I didn't even lay a finger on him.'

'If you had, where would you be now?' Sasous asked. 'In some punishment battalion waiting to be sent for trial?'

'It could have been made to look accidental,' Cato grumbled.

Sasous refuted the suggestion with a snort of disgust. 'With Deval around?' he scoffed. 'Don't be naïve. Deval set you up. He must know about you.'

'He knows all right,' Cato snarled. 'The bastard.'

'To hell with Deval,' Sasous said.

'Sure,' Cato agreed, 'but what about Pedrides? He deserves to be punished. It was my wife, and my son!'

'O.K.,' Sasous agreed. 'Perhaps he deserves to die, but at the right time and in the right place.'

Cato looked up at him.

'Is that what you really want?' Sasous asked. 'Do you really want to have him murdered?'

Cato shook his head. 'I want him brought to justice,' he said.

'So?' Sasous said. 'You set out to prove that he was in the Legion. You have done that. Why not try the official way. Let the authorities know.'

'The authorities!' Cato scoffed. 'They won't want to know. Do you think the Legion would do anything? Or the French Government?'

'Tell your F.B.I. Get all the facts you can about the man. His personal details and background, so that they can be checked. Let the F.B.I. approach the French Government. Pedrides got into the Legion illegally. He can be removed by the Government.' His voice broke into a whisper. Corporal Schnell was walking over to them. 'If the F.B.I. fail,' he said, 'I promise you we can make other arrangements.'

'Stop all the talk, Sasous,' Schnell ordered, 'and get on with the work.'

'Sure, Corporal,' Sasous replied. He started digging.

They worked in silence. The subject was not discussed again that day, but Sasous knew that Cato was thinking over what he had advised him. It was as if he had turned a safety valve inside Cato and released some of his tension and anger. Slowly over the days that followed, Cato began to ease up.

Later that week, Sasous was again able to help Cato. This time by giving him someone else to occupy his thoughts – Jaquie Chauvier! They were in the canteen – exhausted after their day's toil. Larse appeared in his dress uniform. He joined them.

'I have been on duty outside the officers' mess,' he said. 'They are having a dance.'

'Is Deval there?' someone asked.

'Yes,' Larse replied. 'With a most attractive lady.' He made a curvaceous gesture with

118

his hands and kissed his fingers. 'Lucky fellow.'

The subject changed to girls. The men relived some of their more memorable experiences. Sasous turned to Cato. 'You have met Deval's girl friend,' he said.

'Yes,' Cato replied. He gave a half laugh. 'She even invited me to see her here in Djibouti.'

'Then why don't you? We will be given leave this weekend. To hell with Deval.'

To hell with Deval! Sure, Cato thought. To hell with Deval. He took a long drink of wine. Was Jaquie Chauvier Deval's girl friend? he wondered. Was she his mistress? He didn't think so, but did it matter? They were friends – very close friends. But she had certainly invited Cato to visit her. He could remember her words quite clearly, and she had seemed sincere. So why shouldn't he follow it up? It would be one in the eye for Deval. Deval wouldn't like her being friendly with one of his legionnaires. He gave a grunt of satisfaction. Sure, he thought, Deval wouldn't like it. Deval wouldn't like it at all.

'Yeah,' he said. 'Why not? She's Deval's girl friend and to hell with Deval.'

'I'll drink to that,' Sasous smiled.

By the end of the week, Cato had his sights fixed on Pedrides again. He could see the wisdom of Sasous' suggestion and set about building up a dossier on Pedrides to send to the F.B.I. He already knew how Pedrides had got into the Legion, and if he could only get a copy of his new record and background it would give the F.B.I. something to work on. Again Sasous went into action and put the wheels in motion. The clerk in the Adjutant's Office was persuaded to help in return for a financial inducement, and agreed to get a copy of Mandril's file. It was going to take time and patience, but Cato was prepared for both, so long as Mandril was still in the territory.

On their next leave, Cato left the base with Sasous and Raphael, the Gypsy. Sasous was taking Raphael to meet his friends from Paris in their back street bar. Cato spent the afternoon with them, but in the early evening he went to the Hotel Imperial. This time he didn't hesitate outside its imposing entrance and he didn't question his motives. He marched straight up the marble entrance steps and into the lush, cool atmosphere of the hotel foyer. A handful of guests glanced at him with curiosity. He went up to a desk clerk at the reception counter.

'I would like to contact Mademoiselle Chauvier,' he said.

The clerk smiled. 'She does not reside here any longer,' he explained. 'She now has an apartment.'

'Could you give me her address?'

The clerk suddenly remembered something.

'Monsieur Cato?' he asked.

Cato looked surprised. 'Yes,' he said.

'Excuse me one moment, Monsieur.'

The clerk went to a side room and returned with an envelope. 'Mademoiselle left this for you,' he smiled. 'In case you should call.'

He handed Cato the envelope. Cato saw his name written on it, with a note that it was to be collected at some uncertain date. She had been expecting him, he thought, and frowned. He didn't like being taken for granted. He opened the envelope and read a brief message.

'My address is now 157, Rue de Napoleon,' it read. 'Please come and see me.' It was signed, 'Jaquie'.

The message had a friendly ring to it. It made him even more surprised. She really had wanted him to visit her, he thought. He thanked the clerk and took a taxi to the address. It was a modern apartment building in a broad, palm lined boulevard that faced the sea. He found Jaquie Chauvier's name on the fifth floor, but she was not in her apartment. Reluctantly, he retraced his steps and called the elevator.

The elevator came to the ground floor. A number of residents were waiting for it. Cato stepped aside and felt their glances on him. He walked smartly across the terrazzo paved hallway.

'Monsieur Cato!' a woman's voice called out. 'Monsieur Cato!'

Cato stopped, and turned, and saw Jaquie Chauvier. She was wearing a sleeveless, white dress and carrying a bundle of parcels, and she was smiling. Again he felt his heart give a jump. Her smile made her face light up and she looked radiant.

'You got my note?' she asked in English.

'Yes,' he replied.

'I'm glad,' she said.

'Let me take some of your parcels,' he said, uncertain of himself.

She allowed him to take them.

'I've been doing some late shopping,' she explained.

'You look very brown,' he said.

'And you,' she replied. 'How are you finding it?'

'Hot,' he said.

'Me too,' she laughed. 'Come up to my apartment. We can have a cool drink.'

She pressed the elevator call button. She looked genuinely pleased to see him. He wondered why? They had only spoken to each other for such a short while, and yet she behaved as if they were old friends.

'What are you doing?' he asked.

'Working. I can tell you all about the local politics, or the shipping figures for the last two months.'

The elevator appeared.

'I have also learned a lot about the local beliefs and customs,' she smiled. 'All about Allah's will,' she said. 'I've learned about the Koran and how some of the natives can foretell the future.' She looked at him and gave him the smile that lit up her whole face.

'You see, I haven't been just writing columns of gossip. I've been trying to understand the people.'

They came to the fifth floor. They left the elevator and went to her apartment. She opened the door. It was in darkness. The shutters were drawn. She switched on a light. He saw that the room had little furniture. There were two small tables and a few chairs and a handful of ornaments. The floor had bare tiles, and the walls and ceiling were plain white, but it was luxury compared with the barracks.

'I haven't bought a lot of furniture,' she apologised. She turned on a ceiling fan. 'I don't know how long I will be staying.'

'It's like a palace,' he said.

She smiled at the remark and went to her kitchen. She returned with two drinks.

She handed one to him.

'Why did you leave the note?' he asked. He wanted to know. She seemed so genuinely pleased to see him that he was beginning to feel guilty about his original motives in coming to her apartment.

'So that you could contact me,' she said.

'Do you feel sorry for me as a legionnaire, or because of my past?'

She shrugged and returned to the kitchen with her parcels.

'Does it matter why?' she called to him.

'Yes,' he called back. 'It does.'

She rejoined him.

'Why,' she asked. 'Why is it so important?'

He looked away from her.

'I have my reasons,' he said. 'I want to know. Do you feel sorry for me because I am a legionnaire, or because of my past?'

'Couldn't we just leave it that I wish to improve my English?'

He looked up at her.

'I would like to know,' he said. 'Please.'

Her face became serious. She gave a resigned sigh and played with her glass.

'All right,' she said. 'I do know about your past. I was interested in you. Paul Deval knew that. That was why he sent you to my hotel in Bonifacio. He likes doing that sort of thing. Just as he likes finding out about people. When I met you, I liked you, because...' She gesticulated with her hands as she looked for the right words, 'because you are what you are and not because of your past.' She looked away. 'I don't know why these things happen, but they do. There, are you satisfied?'

'Thank you,' he said. 'Thank you.' He knew that she had been honest with him and he was grateful. He also knew that he couldn't use her. Even though she had confirmed his thoughts about Deval. She was too good for Deval.

'Why did Deval find out about me?' he asked.

She shook her head, sadly. 'He is like that. Curious about people, and you were so different from the others.'

She stood up and crossed over to her balcony doorway, and stood looking out to sea.

'He also likes to move people about like pawns of chess,' Cato said.

She turned to face him, abruptly. His tone of contempt had surprised her. There was concern in her eyes.

'What happened?' she asked. 'What happened?'

'Can't you guess?'

There was a moment's silence. 'You came across the man you think killed your family?' she asked.

'I met the man,' Cato said. 'I know it is him. His name is Pedrides.'

'Oh! My God.'

'He came into the Legion by the back door. He uses the name Mandril. I met him face to face, just as Deval had planned, and

I didn't do a thing about it.'

She gave a sigh of relief. 'I'm glad,' she said. 'Very glad.'

'Glad!' he exclaimed. 'Are you? I'm not.' He ran his hand over his short, sandy hair. 'My God! I'm not. I hate myself because I just stood there and looked at him. The man threw a bomb and killed my family and I just walked away from him and threw up. I didn't say anything or do anything.' He looked away. 'I'm ashamed of myself.'

He sat with his head bent. She could see the torment and anguish on his face and she wanted to console him. She wanted to reassure him that Pedrides would get his deserts. That he had been right to walk away from the man. That if he had satisfied his revenge, he would have been brought to a very rough justice. That he would have suffered untold hell. There was such a lot she would have liked to have told him, but she held back. Instead she asked quietly, 'What are you going to do about him?'

He didn't look up at her.

'Somehow I'll see that he is brought to justice,' he whispered. 'I certainly will.'

'Can I help?' she asked. 'I would like to.'

'Perhaps.'

'He'll get his deserts, I just know.'

She had spoken with a feeling that surprised him.

'Do you?' he asked. 'I wish I did.'

They lapsed into silence. The traffic outside made itself heard – a ship in the harbour blasted its siren. Inside the room it was very quiet.

Finally Cato sighed.

'Where is your friend tonight?' he asked.

'He has a social function to attend – a Government function.'

'You going?'

'I declined. I told him that I had some work to do.'

'Have you?'

'If necessary.'

Cato finished his drink and played with the glass in his hands. Suddenly he turned to her.

'You might as well know it all,' he said. 'I hated Deval for bringing me face to face with Pedrides. I hated him nearly as much as I hated myself for my failure. It wasn't the same type of hatred as I have for Pedrides. It was a more personal kind. Deval made me hate myself and that is unforgivable.'

'I understand.'

'I wanted to lash out at him, but I knew that if I touched him, physically, he would have got the better of me. So...' He hesitated. 'I thought you were his girl friend,' he said, and looked away.

'You thought that you would get at Paul through me?' she asked.

'Something like that,' he sighed.

'And now?' she asked.

And now? he wondered. Now he felt disgusted with himself for wanting to use her. It made him almost as bad as Deval, whom he despised.

He shook his head, and picked up his hat.

'If Paul knew that I was entertaining one of his legionnaires after having turned him down,' she said, 'he would be very upset.'

Cato shook his head again. 'It doesn't matter about Deval any more. It doesn't matter at all.'

'No,' she said. 'It doesn't matter, so let's start again.' She came over to him. 'Care for another drink?' she asked.

He looked up at her. She gave him a warm smile. 'And some supper?'

'Sure,' he said. 'So long as I can help.'

'Good.'

Their conflict was over. She collected their glasses and went to the ice box, and returned with more drinks.

'Why did you come out here?' he asked. 'It is so hot, and such a barren country.'

'I lived in Paris,' she explained. 'I have a charming little apartment there, overlooking the Seine. I had my work, and my friends, and a very active social life, but suddenly it all became monotonous. I was repeating myself over and over again. It all seemed rather pointless.' She gave a half laugh. 'This might sound silly, but I became afraid of the future. I knew that I had to do something different. I had to get myself away from my routine. So here I am.' She took a drink and smiled at him. But there was a wistful look in her eyes as if she still had a problem. He saw it and felt sorry for her. Suddenly she was like a young, helpless child a long way from home. She was in Djibouti and to him it was a hell. She deserved something better.

'Something about this place fascinates me,' she said. 'Perhaps it is the harshness – the struggle for survival that the natives have, and the way they accept it. Their fatalism appeals to me. Their belief in Allah is basically the same as ours in God. They say that everything is Allah's will.' She shrugged. 'Perhaps their fatalism is rubbing off on me. Perhaps I think it is God's will that I am here.'

She suddenly brightened up and gave her infectious smile.

'And you are an architect,' she said. 'Tell me about the work you did.'

He told her, and he told her about the bungalow he had designed and built for his family. She encouraged him to talk and she laughed at the amusing incidents in his past and she was serious when he remembered the sad things. But her ready smile was infectious and her personality warm. He couldn't help himself laughing and talking

129

to her, and he couldn't help himself being drawn to her physically.

He was becoming intoxicated by her warmth and delicacy. She was so soft and refined. She was different from the girls that came into the camp – she was like a delicate, scented flower. He was being drawn closer and closer to her. He wanted to touch her fine, long hair and her face, or hold her hand. The feeling became so strong that he abruptly stood up and went to the balcony.

She came up to him. He felt her body close to his.

'What is it?' she asked.

He turned to face her. They were so close that their bodies touched. Gently he put his hand on her face. She took it in her hand and kissed it, and then they had their arms around each other and he was kissing her.

'Come, *chéri*,'she whispered. 'Come.'

She took him to her bedroom and they lay on the soft, scented bed and made love. It was warm, gentle, but fervent love. It was like sailing through a sea of ecstasy, with a gentle breeze that became a wind of passion. And when it was over they lay in each other's arms.

But like the magic of a starry night, there followed the dawn. Cato stirred.

'Do you feel better now?' she whispered.

Better? For a moment Cato had forgotten. He had lived another life, but he was back with himself again.

He moved away from her and sat on the edge of the bed.

'Yes,' he said. 'You helped me to forget for a moment.'

She knelt beside him and leaned her head against his back.

'And you can again.'

'But I will never forget.' He dropped his head. 'I don't want to forget.'

'And you never will, *mon chéri,*'but you can still live again.'

'And with myself?'

He stood up and started to dress. His contempt for himself was back with him again. He had turned away from Pedrides.

'I have to live with myself,' he said.

She saw the set look on his face. He was determined.

'You will,' she said. 'I know you will.'

He hesitated in dressing and looked at her. Their eyes met. He could see that she had faith in him. She believed in him. My God, he thought. He wouldn't turn away from Pedrides again. He wouldn't.

She got a robe and wrapped it around herself. He was fully dressed. They stood looking at each other.

'Will you come back?' she asked.

He didn't know. He wanted to come back, but he knew that if he came back to her he would become involved. She wasn't wanting him to make love to her. She was wanting him back for something deeper.

'It's an easy telephone number to remember,' she said. He glanced down at the 'phone on the stand and read the number.

'Yes, it is,' he agreed.

He went up to her and kissed her gently.

'Thank you,' he said. 'Thank you for everything.' He turned and left her. He knew what she was wanting and he couldn't give it to her, he thought. He hadn't earned the right, and he still had his memories.

He picked up a taxi and rejoined Sasous. Sasous was on his own, sitting at a bar counter where he had been all day. He had a far away look in his eyes. He was back in his Paris. Cato sat alongside him.

'Hullo, *mon ami*,' Sasous drawled, and continued to smoke his cigarette and stare at the back of the bar.

Cato ordered a drink. It arrived.

'Is she nice?' Sasous asked, without turning to him.

'Yes,' Cato said. 'She is very nice.'

'And honest?' Sasous asked. He played with his cigarette. 'Honest and straight?' he asked with a sigh. 'Not a cheat and a liar?'

'No, she is not a cheat and a liar.'

'You are very fortunate then, very fortunate indeed.'

Cato knew that there was more to Sasous' questioning than seeking information about

Jaquie. Sasous had someone else in mind.

'Why do you ask about her character?' he asked. 'How can you ever really know about any woman until you live with them?'

'True,' Sasous agreed, 'and even then, do you ever get to know them.'

They lapsed into silence.

'I lived with a woman,' Sasous said suddenly. 'She was supposed to love me, but all the time she was lying to me and cheating me.' He gripped his glass. Abruptly he picked it up and sank his drink. 'Perhaps deep inside of her she really did love me,' he whispered. 'Perhaps she did. Perhaps she did.'

'What happened, Sasous?' Cato asked. 'Did she let you down?'

Sasous shrugged and ordered another drink. When it arrived he played with the glass.

'She was one of the girls from the club I worked in,' he half whispered. 'She was young, dark, attractive. Collette was her name. We lived together, but all the time we were living together she was informing the *pigs*. One night we had a big job planned. Collette knew about it. She got me to make love to her, and she fixed my drink. I didn't go on the job. I was asleep. The *pigs* picked up two of my friends – two others were killed, as they tried to escape.'

His head got nearer to the glass. 'It was all

my fault,' he said. 'I should never have talked. I should not have trusted Collette.'

'Perhaps she did really love you, Sasous,' Cato said. 'She tried to protect you.'

Sasous shook his head.

'She lost me my honour,' he said. 'That is unforgivable.'

'They couldn't blame you,' Cato said. 'It was not really your doing.'

'They blamed the girl,' Sasous said, tight lipped, 'and she paid the price.'

Cato put his arm on his friend's shoulder. Sasous was almost over the hill. The proprietor motioned with his head. Cato moved closer to him.

'I heard him telling you his story,' he whispered. 'The girl was found dead in the Seine, and he…' He moved his head fractionally, to indicate Sasous. 'He was banished from Paris. If he ever returns, he will join the girl.'

Cato had guessed as much.

'We need a taxi,' he said.

'There is a number on the wall above the telephone.'

Cato went to the 'phone. He ordered the taxi and went back to the bar. Sasous' head was on the counter. He was sleeping peacefully.

Another soldier staggered into the bar. He wasn't a legionnaire, but he had the same drilled, disciplined look about him and his pleasures were similar to those of the

134

legionnaires. He wanted drink and women. Cato watched him and scowled to himself. He could end up just like the soldier if he didn't keep contact with the outside world, he thought. He would spend his leaves in bars like the one he was in, or at brothels like Rosie's. But Jaquie had shown him a different side of life. It was the type of life that he had been used to. He had to hang on to that. He had to. He went back to the telephone and dialled Jaquie's number. Jaquie answered the call straight away as if she had been sitting by the 'phone. The sound of her voice made him feel warm inside.

'This is Lee,' he said.

There was no delay. 'I was hoping you would ring.'

'I would like to come around again,' he said.

'I'll be waiting for you,' she said. 'I'm so pleased.'

'Thanks,' he said. 'Goodnight.'

'Not goodnight – *au revoir.*'

'Yes, *au revoir.*'

TEN

The anticipation of combat that had been constantly under the surface, suddenly became a reality, and Deval got his opportunity to realise his ambition.

The French Government had suddenly become alarmed. Hakim's name was being mentioned in diplomatic circles. His friends in the East had started a campaign to make his cause known. The French Government knew that they had to act swiftly. They couldn't afford to let Hakim's cause take root. They didn't want another Indo-China, or Algeria, on their hands. Hakim had to be dealt with immediately. The Military Commander in Djibouti was ordered to act decisively, swiftly and secretively. There was to be no world press publicity; no opportunity for a call to the United Nations; no mention of hostilities; no recognition of Abdul Hakim as a freedom fighter. Abdul Hakim and his cause had to cease to exist.

The men greeted the news philosophically. They were legionnaires trained to fight and kill, and the Legion was always the first into action. They set about their preparations.

Cato was equally philosophical. He didn't know what to expect or what lay ahead. He accepted each day as it came. He was now back on an even keel again, thanks to Jaquie and Sasous. He hadn't seen Jaquie again, but he often thought about her, and Sasous was making good progress. Soon Cato would have all the information he needed to send to the F.B.I.

On the evening before they were due to move out, Cato was on *sentinelle* duty. When he had finished his tour of duty, and was leaving the *poste*, Larse joined him. They walked to the barracks together.

'I was wanting to talk to you, Cato,' Larse said, in a tone of voice that suggested that he had something to discuss of a secret nature. '*The Gypsy* has had another premonition,' he added.

He always referred to Raphael as *The Gypsy*, whenever the subject was connected with Raphael's clairvoyancy. Otherwise he was still Raphael.

'He hasn't spoken of it,' Cato said.

'He never does unless it is good news.'

Cato looked at Larse.

'*The Gypsy* forecasts that you are going to *travel*, Cato,' Larse whispered.

Cato didn't reply. He knew that Larse meant that *The Gypsy* was forecasting that Cato was going to quit the Legion – to desert. It was something that he would not have denied, except for two persons – Pedrides and Sasous. So long as Pedrides was alive and in the territory, he would remain. After he had seen Pedrides brought to justice, he would think again. Perhaps then he might *travel,* but a lot would depend on Sasous and Sasous' own plans for the future.

'I come from Lillehammer,' Larse added. 'My father owns a sports shop. I used to help him, but I thought it was too boring. I wanted adventure, so here I am.'

'Why are you telling me this?' Cato asked.

'I have only two more years to serve to fulfil my commitment,' Larse explained. 'After that I will return to Norway and settle down. I would like to keep in contact with you, Cato. Perhaps you will look me up sometime.'

Cato stopped in his tracks. Larse did likewise.

'You really do believe in *The Gypsy's* forecasts?' Cato asked.

'Yes,' Larse replied. 'I do. He seems to have this gift.'

'What else did he foretell?' Cato asked.

Larse shrugged. 'He thinks that there is going to be a lot of killing, but he hasn't spelled it out, and I haven't asked.'

They walked on again. Cato liked Larse. He was an adventurer like many other legionnaires, and he was uncomplicated. There was nothing devious about him, or his past, and there was nothing troubling him, and he was obviously a great believer in *The Gypsy*.

'Well,' Cato said. 'I don't know whether I believe *The Gypsy* or not, but if it does come true, I will certainly contact you and keep in touch.'

'That's good, Cato. I'll give you the address.'

They came to the barrack block. Some of the men were in the canteen, others were getting their equipment ready for the move. Sasous was waiting for Cato. They went to the canteen together.

'I hear *The Gypsy* has been forecasting your future,' Sasous remarked, as they approached the canteen.

'So Larse was telling me. Do you believe such people like *The Gypsy* can be clairvoyant?'

Sasous shrugged. 'I have learned not to disbelieve such people,' he said.

'Has he told you anything?'

'He doesn't have to. I know I will not see Paris again.'

Cato opened his mouth to protest.

'Don't worry yourself,' Sasous intervened. 'I don't any longer.'

They entered the canteen. It was busy and crowded, but the atmosphere was subdued. Often there was a strong feeling of comradeship in the canteen. That night was one of them. A group of Polish legionnaires started singing some of their folk songs. Their singing was melodious and moving. The other legionnaires listened and drank. Cato and Sasous sat together, but Sasous sat with his thoughts. He was back in his Paris. He had his own premonition about his future.

ELEVEN

At dawn, the men were paraded and inspected. They wore full battle order, with four grenades strapped to their webbing. Their only concession was that they were allowed to wear their bush hats, in lieu of their steel helmets, but they had their steel helmets and their white *képis* in their packs. They were prepared for combat.

The men were assigned to their various vehicles. Cato and Sasous were detailed to Deval's long range reconnaissance car. It was a large, cumbersome, open vehicle, equipped with a machine gun and radio, that could be driven anywhere.

Captain Kubik's Section was the first to leave the camp. Their area of search was to the north of the territory and they had the greatest distance to cover. They were returning to the *poste* that Cato had previously visited – the *poste* where Pedrides was stationed. Cato knew this as they drove west, but Pedrides didn't trouble him as he had before. He was determined that he wouldn't walk away from him again, but he wouldn't purposely confront him neither. He would deal with Pedrides the official way first.

141

There was also a feeling about their move that suggested to him that the events that were to follow were going to be of greater consequence than his personal battle with Pedrides. He saw the glint in Deval's eyes as Deval sat staring at the horizon in front of them, and knew that Deval also had a feeling about the outcome of their move.

In the mid afternoon they reached the *poste*. Sasous gave Cato an anxious glance. He was thinking the same as Cato. Was Pedrides back in the *poste*, but he was also wondering how would Cato react? Cato gave a faint smile and shook his head telling his friend not to concern himself.

The legionnaires at the *poste* were sullen and quiet. Cato soon learned why. Four legionnaires had been killed the previous day. A scout car on patrol in the mountains had exploded. Nobody knew why, but everybody suspected a mine or a booby trap. The four men in the vehicle had been killed instantly. There was strong resentment amongst the men of the station and the natives were being uncooperative. They were not talking. A barrier was developing. There was trouble in the wind.

In the evening a helicopter hovered, briefly, over the *poste* and landed on the plain close by. Two staff officers and two native scouts got out and hurried into the camp.

After it had turned dark, the Section was

suddenly ordered to parade in battle order. The men had anticipated the order. They hurriedly put on their equipment and collected their packs and rifles. As Cato left the barrack room, he saw Larse. He went over to him.

'*Bon chance, mon ami,*' Larse said, and gripped his arm.

'And you also, Larse,' Cato replied.

They quickly shook hands. They would be going different ways and there was *The Gypsy's* forecast.

They joined the parade. Captain Kubik addressed his Section. Lieutenant Deval stood by his side.

'Our orders are to search the mountain range to the north to seek out a band of terrorists lead by Abdul Hakim,' he said. 'Somewhere in the mountains he has his base. Other units are looking for him along the mountain range to the south. When we locate his position, the main force will be flown in and we will engage Hakim's men in combat. We will move out immediately. At day break we will reach Kafar Wadi where there is an outpost and a fuel dump. We will then divide into three Sections. Number one Section will scout the mountains south of the dump and return to the *poste.* Sergeant Trocco will command that Section. Number two Section, under my command, will patrol the pass at the wadi and the mountains to the north. Number three Section will patrol to the northern limits of the territory under the command of Monsieur, Lieutenant Deval.' The Captain paused. 'This is not a training exercise,' he said sternly, 'but we do not fight unless we have to. Our orders are to search and trail, but if we are engaged in action, we shoot to kill.' He turned to Sergeant Bouchier. 'Carry on,' he ordered.

Bouchier saluted the Captain and turned to his men.

'If anybody fails me,' he warned, his eyes menacingly searching the ranks for possible failures, 'I will deal with them personally.' He smacked his cane into the palm of his gloved hand and eyed the men. 'When you dismiss, get into your vehicles. And be sharp about it. *Rompez!*'

The men fell out and boarded their vehicles. Cato joined Sasous in Deval's scout car. They found one of the native scouts already aboard. He was a tall, slim man, with large, round eyes, that seemed to light up in the moonlight. He was dressed in a long, white robe and headscarf. He greeted the men with a flashing smile, that contrasted so vividly with his ebony coloured face.

'Me – Habra Zugja,' he said. 'I speak very good French.'

'O.K. Zugi,' Sasous said, purposefully making the native's name more easily pronounceable. 'I am Sasous. This is Berge and Cato and Diago.' He introduced the group. The native scout repeated each of their names and gave them a flashing smile. The men returned the greeting and called him Zugi. From then on he was to be Zugi to them, and he liked it.

'Where are we going, Zugi?' Diago asked.

Zugi bared his white teeth in a huge grin.

'To the mountains,' he said. 'Far to the north.'

'Plenty of bang! bang!' Diago asked.

Zugi smiled. 'If it is so written,' he beamed.

Lieutenant Deval boarded the vehicle. Berge started the engine. The men sat silent. Sasous played with his radio and there was the inevitable jumble of noises as he tuned the set.

'Keep your calls to a minimum,' Deval ordered. 'The terrorists also have their radios.'

That was the first indication that the men had been given that the terrorists were not anything more than a bunch of dissident natives. Diago looked at Cato and raised his eyebrows in acknowledgement of the information.

The convoy drove out of the *poste* and headed north. They followed the track used by the reconnaissance patrols, but they were driving without headlights. It was an uncomfortable journey. The moon gave a dull, yellow glow and cast long, dark shadows that hid the bumps and depressions in their path. Sasous gave up his radio link with the control vehicles and concentrated on keeping his equipment intact and in position.

The night passed slowly and the men wrapped their blankets around themselves as the cold night breeze chilled their bodies.

Soon, after dawn, they came to the outpost at Kafar Wadi. A fire was burning by a cookhouse and a legionnaire stood by the stove. Two other legionnaires were on *sentinelle* at the lookouts. Cato couldn't stop himself from looking for Pedrides, but he saw no sign of him, and the convoy only halted long enough for Captain Kubik to confer with Lieutenant Deval.

The three groups went their respective ways. Lieutenant Deval's unit had three vehicles – two reconnaissance cars and a stores truck. Sergeant Bouchier was in command of the second reconnaissance vehicle. Hessler was driving. With them were Irish, Hook and Napoleon. Corporal Schnell was in charge of the stores vehicle. Vasey was driving. In the rear were Fritz, Greco and Boussec. Fritz had been detailed to be in charge of the stores and Greco, much to his dislike, had been detailed to act as cook. Greco was a good cook. It had been his trade before he had turned revolutionary, but the detail didn't seem to please him. None of the men were talkative. The hot wind was for ever blowing the dust at them and the sun shone down from a furnace that seemed to be directly over their heads. There was also Hakim to think of.

Deval suffered the discomfort with an inner awareness that his plans were going to unfold before him. There was no logical reason to think that Hakim would be in the mountains to the north. The railway that had often been his target in the past was much further south. But Deval sensed that fate was leading him to his destiny. He was convinced that it was not intended that he should sweat and endure the rigours of the Legion and just grow old. He felt that something great was destined for him, and he was going to find it on that reconnaissance.

They drove all morning and afternoon, resting only at certain landmarks on Deval's map, when he would check and re-check his bearings. Several times, as they journeyed, they saw tribes of nomads with their trail of camels plodding slowly towards the watering points in the mountains, and Zugi, the interpreter, would always be eager to explain something about their movements, or the terrain. Unfortunately, Deval didn't encourage him to talk and would brusquely order him to be quiet. At one of the halts,

147

Sasous did speak to him.

'If your country ever became indepen-
dent, Zugi,' he said, with a glint in his eyes.
'What will they make you?'

Zugi took the question in the right spirit.

'A General,' he said, his eyes wide and his
face a picture of pride. 'General Zugja,' he
said proudly, 'and, if not me, then my
children, or my children's children.'

'Because the French have educated you,'
Cato pointed out.

'That is so,' Zugi agreed. 'I am grateful to
them. That is why I serve them. I will not
fight against them. I will wait for Allah's
call.'

'Zugja!'

It was Sergeant Bouchier. Zugi responded
quickly. He rushed over to him.

'Not Allah's call, yet,' Sasous smiled, 'but
nevertheless, one to be immediately obeyed.'

He returned to the vehicle to re-arrange
some of his radio stores. Diago and the
others went to the stores truck. Cato continued to study the shimmering waves of
heat that quivered across the plain.

'The desert has always presented a challenge to man,' a voice said. It was Lieutenant
Deval!

Cato turned abruptly. He hadn't heard the
Lieutenant come up to him. Deval was
replacing his compass in its case. There was
a smile on his lips. This was the first time

that he had addressed Cato since the incident with Pedrides.

'Or does man bring his own challenge to the desert?' Deval asked.

Cato saw the glint of amusement in his eyes. It was the incident with Pedrides all over again, he thought. Deval was thinking of Pedrides. He felt himself flush up, but controlled his anger.

'So long as they are not contrived, *mon Lieutenant*, I will accept any challenges.'

'As Allah's will?' Deval asked, with amusement.

'Perhaps.'

It was out in the open now, Cato thought. Straight down the line. There were no holds barred.

'He has brought some very interesting people to this territory,' Cato said. 'Perhaps he might leave some behind, *mon Lieutenant*.'

Deval's face broke into a smile again. Cato's remark appealed to him.

'You're a romantic, legionnaire,' he said, and returned to his vehicle. Sasous sidled up to Cato.

'What was all that about?' he whispered.

'An unfriendly bit of cross talk,' Cato replied. 'I think I would prefer to be left alone with Sergeant Bouchier, than our dear Lieutenant. He reminds me of a snake.'

'Get aboard!' Bouchier shouted. 'Pronto! Pronto!'

149

The men rejoined their vehicles, and covered themselves with their head scarfs.

The convoy continued its patrol. Late in the afternoon they saw just how grim the terrain could be. In the distance they saw the tell-tale sign of a hovering flock of vultures. They were circling the sky and suddenly swooping to the ground to attack their victim. The men watched them silently and sullenly.

Hook withdrew his rifle from its rack.

'Leave it!' Bouchier ordered. 'Their victim will be dead.'

But their victim was not dead. As they drove closer to the object of the vultures' attention, they saw the emaciated shape of a camel lying on the ground. Its humps were lumps of skin. But it was not dead!

'Mon Dieu!' Diago hissed. 'Even a camel dies of thirst in this place.'

'The camel has been left,' Zugi hurriedly explained, 'because it could not keep up with the train. The vultures attack it until they kill it. They go for the eyes first.'

The men looked at the poor creature's eyes. One of them was hanging out of its sunken socket where the vultures had picked at it. Deval ordered Bouchier to shoot the half dead beast. Bouchier told Hook. Hook got his rifle and jumped out of his vehicle and fired two shots into the beast's head. He quickly fired two more into the sky at the

flying vultures. One fell to the ground.
'That's enough!' Bouchier yelled. He turned on Hook. 'You do anything without my orders again and I'll stake you to the ground for the vultures to pick at,' he said, and sank his cane into Hook's stomach. 'Now get back in the vehicle,' he shouted.

Hook scowled and returned to his scout car.

'Where would the tribe be making for?' Deval asked Zugi.

'For the mountains, *mon Lieutenant* – *Sahib*,' Zugi replied.

'Is there a pass near here?' Deval asked. He looked at the mountains. He could see no pass.

'There is the remains of an ancient town to the north,' Zugi explained. 'There is a watering hole and a valley in which to graze cattle.'

'But there is no pass?'

'I do not know of a pass, *Sahib*.'

'How far away is this valley?'

Zugi shrugged. 'About half a day's march,' he said.

'Only half a day,' Deval mused. 'Then why did they leave their camel?'

'It was dying, *Sahib*,' Zugi replied.

Deval turned to him. 'Half a day from water,' he said. 'They would not leave a camel. Unless...?' He looked at Zugi for an answer.

'They were in a hurry, Sahib,' Zugi said eagerly.

Deval didn't reply. He looked at his map. 'Where is this place?'

Zugi studied the mountains, thoughtfully, for a full two minutes. Then he pointed his arm to one of the peaks.

'It is in that direction, Sahib,' he said.

Deval took a bearing and referred to his map.

He gave Berge a new course. The convoy turned and went in the direction Zugi had indicated – towards the mountains. The men looked at their destination and then turned away. The mountains looked as un-inviting as the plain and they could see no valley. But the inlet to the valley was hidden in the shadow of a projecting spur. It was only when they were upon it that they saw its entrance. They drove along a river wadi and through the inlet with the mountain sides towering over them on both sides, and suddenly they were in the valley. The con-trast almost took their breath away. From a hard crusted, yellow, dusty river bed they had suddenly entered into a flat, bottle-shaped valley that had a faint colour of green about it. Across the floor of the valley was a coarse grass and a variety of shrubs and trees that crept up the terraced forward slopes of the mountains before becoming part of the yellow rocks and scree. Some of the trees had green stalks. All of them were strange, unusual shapes. Amongst them were the usual gnarled, fig trees, but at the head of the valley was a circle of palm trees around a water hole. And there were flocks of sheep, and herds of camels, grazing on the slopes, that didn't look half emaciated.

Deval brought the convoy to a halt and the men immediately felt the silence. It was a strange, eerie, silence. It was as if the mountains had shut out all sound. It made the men feel uneasy. The dust had settled and they saw the sheep and camels and native herdsmen standing like statues amongst their beasts. They saw also the ruins of an old town at the head of the valley – a pattern of stone walls that had once been the foundations of a small community. But it was the silence and the towering mountains that the men noticed most of all. The mountains seemed to crowd in on them after the openness of the plain. Their irregular shapes reached far into the sky and their peaks were hidden from their view.

'Where are the people?' Deval asked.

'In the caves, *Sahib*,' Zugi replied. 'They live in the caves at the head of the valley, on the terraces, beside the ruins of the town.'

Deval examined them through his binoculars. He saw the caves up the sides of the mountains and the dark skinned tribespeople emerging from them like ants from the

153

ground. He also saw a saddle in the mountain range behind the row of cave dwellings that looked like a pass into the valley beyond.

'Are they friendly?' he asked. The men listened for Zugi's reply.

'But certainly, *Sahib*,' Zugi assured him. 'All the tribespeople are friendly. It is only Hakim with his lies and promises, that brings disgrace upon my people.' He stuck out his chest proudly. 'We will find Hakim,' he added, 'and we will kill him.'

'And the saddle? Is it a pass?'

'I do not know, *Sahib*.'

Sergeant Bouchier reported to Deval for his orders.

'We will camp here tonight,' Deval said.

Bouchier gave the orders and the men set about their tasks. Lieutenant Deval sat in his vehicle silently studying the figures on the hillside. He called Sergeant Bouchier and Zugi to him.

'I want you to go and speak to the Sultan,' he ordered Zugi. 'Give him my greetings and tell him that we will be staying one night, but we will not use his water hole. Ask him if he knows of Hakim's whereabouts.'

'Yes, *Sahib*.'

Deval turned to Sergeant Bouchier. 'Send Corporal Schnell with him,' he ordered, 'and tell him to keep his eyes open.'

'He will, *mon Lieutenant*.'

Bouchier gave Corporal Schnell his orders,

and the Corporal and Zugi left their camp at a trot. The men watched them, as they worked.

'Can these natives be trusted, Cato?' Irish asked, when they had set up camp.

'You can never tell with them,' Cato replied.

'We have the machine guns,' Vasey said.

'They have the numbers,' Hook pointed out. He wiped some dust from his face. 'This bloody place,' he growled. The dust had caused a sore to appear on his face. It was giving him trouble. It made him more surly than before.

'Hakim is not in these parts,' Boussec said.

'How do you bloody well know?' Hook growled. 'Has he told you his plans?'

Boussec looked apologetic. 'You said it was too far from the railway.'

'Well, I've changed my bloody mind,' Hook grunted. 'Perhaps he isn't bloody well interested in the bloody railway. Perhaps he is just collecting his bloody friends together.'

'Here is the Corporal and Zugi,' someone called out.

Zugi and Corporal Schnell came trotting back to the camp. Zugi wasn't smiling and his face looked perplexed. He reported to Deval.

'The Sultan is Mohammed Hajr,' he said. 'His family has used this water hole for generations. He will be pleased for you to stay as long as you wish.'

That was a customary courtesy amongst the tribespeople, which gave Deval no true indication of the Sultan's attitude.

'Is he friendly?' he asked.

'He is a Somali from the south, *Sahib,* like Hakim,' Zugi replied, with an apologetic air, 'and they have had a hard summer.'

'They do not blame us for that?' Deval suggested.

'They know it is Allah's will, *Sahib,*' Zugi replied.

'You haven't answered my question. Are they friendly?'

'They are a mixed tribe, *Sahib.* That is unusual. I saw some Afars and Somalis. There is also a Yibir elder with them.'

'A Yibir!' Deval exclaimed. He knew the tribe of Yibir was known for their practice of black magic.

'They are sorcerers and practice witch-craft, *Sahib.*'

'And Hakim uses them,' Deval retorted.

'These people are not unfriendly, *Sahib,*' Zugi said. 'So long as they are left alone to use their water hole.'

'And Hakim?'

'They have heard of him like they have heard of the mountain lion, *Sahib,* and they fear him as they fear the lion.'

Deval was not impressed.

'Is he in these parts?'

'They do not know, *Sahib*.'

Deval turned his attention to Corporal Schnell.

'They appear well fed and clothed, *mon Lieutenant*,' Schnell reported. 'And they are suspicious of us.'

'Any signs of any weapons?'

'No, *mon Lieutenant*.'

'Well clothed and well fed,' Deval said, 'and it has been a hard summer.'

He turned to Sergeant Bouchier who was standing alongside him.

'I would very much like to search their caves,' he said.

This time Zugi's concern came bubbling forth.

'That would cause great trouble, *Sahib*,' he pleaded. 'Big trouble. They are very proud people.'

Deval frowned. He didn't like anyone talking out of turn. He abruptly dismissed Zugi and Corporal Schnell, and stood with Sergeant Bouchier.

'We will leave tomorrow for the sea and return later,' he ordered. 'Perhaps we might surprise them.'

'You think that they are linked with Hakim, *mon Lieutenant*?' Bouchier asked.

Deval shrugged. 'They are better fed and equipped than this valley would normally provide,' he said. 'I would dearly like to search the village.'

'Zugja was right,' Bouchier warned. 'It could cause trouble. We have no excuse.'

'Unfortunately not,' Deval agreed. He shook his head. 'I would still like to know why they are so well fed.'

He dismissed his Sergeant. Bouchier returned to the men. Greco had a meal prepared. Fritz was tidying the cooking quarters. The others were cleaning their rifles and resting. They were all unusually quiet.

'What's the matter with you all?' Bouchier snapped. 'You are like a lot of frightened girls.' He expanded his chest. 'I want some noise,' he ordered. 'I want some laughter, and I want some music and singing.' His eyes scanned their faces. 'I don't want them to think we are suspicious of them,' he growled. 'I want them to think we are happy. Do you understand? Talk! Sing!'

'Yes, Sergeant.'

'Well, talk!'

Reluctantly, Cato and the men did as Bouchier ordered. Their original lack of enthusiasm had not been brought up by any awe of the natives who they pitied more than feared. It was the cumulative effect of the oppressive heat, the flies, the mosquitos, and the dust that had sapped their energy, and they felt that the strange, eerie silence that hung over the valley was because every living creature in it had suffered the same during the long, hot day.

Lieutenant Deval remained aloof. He had his own flask of brandy. He sat beside his vehicle, and watched the flickering light from the native fires. He wondered why the natives had left the camel to die so close to their village. Why they had been in such a hurry. It troubled him. There was something going on. He could sense it, but he couldn't get to grips with it.

Bouchier also sensed trouble. He stood smacking his cane against his gloved hand. He considered doubling the guards, but decided against it. No one would disturb them, he thought, or come close. Not with a sentry and their camp fires.

The men sang and talked, but as the cold air crept over the valley, the singing died away and they settled into their bedrolls close to the fires. The camp fires and lights of the native settlement went out, one by one, and a stillness settled over the valley.

The men slept and the night passed peacefully, but as dawn approached a voice suddenly called out in panic.

'Sergeant! My rifle! It has gone!' The cry had come from Boussec. Everyone was immediately awake.

'*Aux armes!*' Bouchier ordered, loudly. 'Take cover!'

The men grabbed their rifles.

Bouchier turned, angrily, on Boussec.

'What do you mean, missing?' he growled. He stood scowling at him. The others were standing to, fully alert.

'I had my rifle by my side when I came off guard duty,' Boussec stammered. 'It's gone!'

'Who took over from you?'

'Vasey, Sergeant,' Boussec replied, nervously.

'Vasey!' Bouchier hissed. 'Vasey!' he yelled. 'Come here.'

Vasey moved towards Bouchier. His pace was slow and hesitant like an animal that was going to receive a beating.

'You took over from Boussec,' Bouchier shouted. 'He had his rifle when you took over. He hasn't got it now.'

Vasey got the gist of what the Sergeant was implying.

'I patrolled the area during my tour, Sergeant,' he said, picking his words.

Sergeant Bouchier mimicked him. 'You patrolled the area during your tour,' he scoffed. His eyes became enflamed. 'Somebody got in and took a rifle,' he shouted. 'You let somebody get through. You incompetent idiot!'

Vasey flushed up at the Sergeant's abuse.

'Nobody got through when I was on duty, Sergeant,' he growled.

'Nobody?' Bouchier asked. He swung around to the rest of the men. 'All of you,' he shouted. 'You had better find the rifle, or

160

else.' He turned back to Vasey and Boussec. 'I'll peg you both to the ground if it isn't found. Do you understand? Nobody loses a rifle! Nobody! Look for it. All of you – look for it.'

They started looking.

Deval slowly got out of his bedroll and adjusted his clothing.

'Sergeant Bouchier!' he called out.

Bouchier went to him.

'Boussec has lost his rifle, *mon Lieutenant*,' Bouchier reported. 'If he doesn't find it, I'll peg him out for the vultures.'

'Could one of the natives have taken it?' Deval asked.

'They could,' Bouchier grunted.

'In which case we will have to search their village,' Deval said, with a glint in his eyes.

'Yes, *mon Lieutenant*,' Bouchier agreed.

'Zugja!' Deval called out.

The native guide reported to him.

'We have lost a rifle,' Deval said. 'It has been stolen. Go and tell the Sultan what has happened. Tell him that if the rifle is not handed back in fifteen minutes we will search his village.'

'Oh, no, *Sahib*,' Zugi said with alarm. 'They will not like that. It will not be good.'

'In which case they will return the rifle,' Deval said. 'Go and tell the Sultan.'

Zugi moved away. Deval turned to Bouchier. 'Get the men ready,' he ordered.

161

'I want a thorough search made.' He looked into Bouchier's eyes. 'A thorough search, Sergeant,' he added. 'I want to know why those natives are so well fed and clothed. I want to know what they have in their caves.'

Bouchier got the message. The Lieutenant was going to take the opportunity of satisfying his curiosity about other matters as well.

'I understand, *mon Lieutenant,*' he said.

'Good. We will move straight away.'

'The fifteen minutes' grace?' Bouchier asked.

'It will take that long for us to reach the village.'

Bouchier returned to the men and gave his orders. The men looked uncertain. They had never forcibly entered a native dwelling before.

'You move in threes,' Bouchier ordered. 'One man stands guard outside the dwelling, one man stands guard inside, and the third does the search. I want to know what they have in their caves. What weapons they have, what food they have. Do you understand?'

They understood.

'Greco, Fritz. You stay and guard the stores and the transport. Berge, you drive the Lieutenant's vehicle. We take one reconnaissance car. You stay with it and have the machine gun ready for action.' He turned to the other men. 'Move it! Pronto!'

The men moved. Berge drove the scout car towards the head of the valley with Sergeant Bouchier and Lieutenant Deval alongside him. The men marched, led by Corporal Schnell. It was dawn, but the word had quickly spread around the native encampment. They could see the natives coming out of their caves. The Sultan and a party of elders stood arguing with Zugi on the terrace above the ruins of the town. Lieutenant Deval remained with Berge in the scout car at the foot of the incline that faced the natives' caves. Berge positioned himself at the mounted machine gun. The party of elders approached the Lieutenant. As Zugi pleaded their cause, Bouchier gave out his orders. The men went in threes and quickly started their search.

Cato was with Napoleon and Hook. Reluctantly, he entered a beehive hut on the forward slopes. He saw the pitiful possessions of the natives – the straw mats, the meagre cooking utensils, the frightened look in the children's eyes, and he felt the anger of the men folk. It hung heavy in the morning air. For Cato it was an unpleasant duty. The stench of bodies and animals, and excreta, offended the sensitivity of his nostrils and stomach. They were stenches that he was not used to. Nor was he used to the primitive conditions of wattle huts and caves with utensils of a primitive age. The natives lived like animals. He felt sorry for them, and in sympathy with their resentment.

The three men took turn about in their drill. Hook was not so offended by the stench or so sensitive to the natives. He gruffly moved their belongings and scattered them around their living quarters. Napoleon also took a delight in the search. He enjoyed the drama of disturbing the people in their quarters – particularly the women in their beds. One disturbance brought particular delight to him, but nearly caused a riot.

They were searching a cave. Its entrance was covered by a matting that acted both as a door and a camouflage. Cato was on guard outside the cave. A group of native men had gathered around and stood watching. Suddenly there was a woman's shriek from inside the cave. It was a short, sharp cry of fear. Cato gripped his automatic rifle as the group of native men moved towards him. They stopped in front of him. There was a silence and then the sound of scuffling from inside the cave. Nobody came out. There was another cry. Again the natives moved, and Cato gesticulated with his rifle. He moved the entrance flap to one side. At a glance, he saw what was happening. A young native woman lay naked on a bed. Her copper coloured body was curled up for protection. Standing leering over her was Napoleon. In his hand was the blanket that had been covering the woman's body. The woman's husband was being held to the ground by Hook. Napoleon threw away the blanket. The man on the ground struggled. Hook held him back.

'Go on, Napoleon,' Hook shouted. 'Let's see you *poof!*'

The girl whimpered and cringed. Hook laughed again. 'Go on!' he urged.

'Make one more move, Napoleon,' Cato said, 'and so help me, I will kill you!'

There was an immediate, pregnant silence. Napoleon turned to see Cato with his rifle pointing at him. Hook also turned.

'What's the matter?' Hook sneered. 'Have you not got the stomach for a bit of native?'

'Let him go, Hook, or I will shoot you also.'

Suddenly, Sergeant Bouchier burst in amongst them.

'What the hell's going on?' he shouted.

He didn't need an explanation.

'Get back to the camp, Napoleon,' he ordered. 'And you, Hook. Move it!'

Napoleon left the cave. Hook gave Cato a look of hatred and also departed.

'Don't think you'll get any thanks from the natives,' Bouchier blazed at Cato. 'Or the Lieutenant.'

He swung around and left the cave. Cato picked up the blanket from the ground. As he did so, he saw a row of small sacks of grain beside the girl. She had been lying on them, her body covering them. He threw the blanket over her and turned to leave. He saw the dark face of her husband. It had two deep scars down each cheek. There was no look of gratitude in his eyes, only defiance and hatred. Cato looked away and left the cave. A group of natives eyed him sullenly. They were standing all around the hillside watching the search, with a look of resentment and defiance on their faces. Cato returned to the reconnaissance vehicle where Lieutenant Deval was watching the search. Napoleon and Hook were walking back to the camp. Cato reported to the Lieutenant. Deval continued to watch the search. Cato waited patiently.

'What have you seen?' Deval asked.

'They have sacks of grain, *mon Lieutenant*,' Cato replied. 'Small sacks that can be carried by hand.'

'Sacks. Any markings?'

'None, but they are well provided.'

Deval grunted. 'It appears to confirm my thinking,' he said. 'Any weapons?'

'Very few, *mon Lieutenant*.'

'That's strange. They have weapons. They must have. Yet they keep them hidden.'

'They might have a central armoury.'

'The weapons are precious,' Deval said, more to himself than to Cato. 'They probably expected us to search their camp, so they will have hidden them somewhere. It is a pity that we cannot question one of them more closely.'

Cato saw a frown appear on the Lieutenant's face and wondered what was going through his mind. The Lieutenant turned his back on him. Cato was being dismissed without any reference being made to the incident in the cave. It was obvious that Deval wasn't concerned.

Cato moved away. The patrols started returning. They had found only a few rifles and no ammunition, but they had seen the grain in the small sacks.

Deval ordered Bouchier to take him back to camp. The men returned on foot. Questions were asked about Hook and Napoleon. Cato explained what had happened.

'Hook is an animal,' Diago hissed. 'So is Napoleon.'

'What do you think will happen to them?' Irish asked.

'*Monsieur Le Lieutenant* has his mind too occupied with Hakim to worry about Hook and Napoleon,' Fritz said.

His words were proved to be correct. Deval listened to the various reports from the men and to Bouchier's report of the incident.

'Perhaps a little over-zealousness on everybody's part,' Deval said. 'This is the men's first experience of a search?'

'Yes, *mon Lieutenant*,' Bouchier replied.

'You deal with them, Sergeant, and by the way – I found the rifle. It was in the bushes close to where the men were sleeping.'

He handed Bouchier the rifle. Bouchier accepted it with only a fleeting look of surprise on his face. If he had any thoughts about Deval's actions, he didn't show them. He went over to Hook and Napoleon and gave them a dressing down that warned them that the matter could be brought up again if Bouchier so decided. In the course of his abuse his cane lashed into both men in places where it hurt most. When he was finished they both slunk away and remained aloof from the rest of the men.

Greco gave out the breakfast. The men ate it eagerly, but the word had got around about Boussec's rifle. They knew that Deval had tricked them and they quietly cursed his guts. There had been no need for the deceit. They would have searched the natives' quarters without his trickery. Deval had miscalculated. He had shown them that he was twisted and devious. He had conjured up an excuse for his own conscience. There was something sick about Deval. It was then that another title for Deval was whispered around the men. It was *Le Serpent* – *the Snake* – the twisted one!

The men finished their meal and broke

camp. Deval sat in his vehicle and studied his maps.

'Those tribespeople are up to something,' Bouchier growled to the men. 'They could be linked with Hakim. We aren't going to find out sitting on our arses and they are too smart to let us wander around their camps. We are going north for a couple of days. Then we will return suddenly at night and catch them unawares.' He gave a grin of satisfaction. Like Deval, he was enjoying the situation. The men saw it on his face. His words confirmed it. 'You scum might see some action, after all,' he said. 'Then we'll see just how tough you all are.' His eyes held Vasey, momentarily. 'I shall enjoy watching you all perform,' he said, 'and I don't mean *poofing.*' His face hardened. 'Now move it!– Pronto!'

They moved it.

TWELVE

The three vehicles left the valley and headed north again, skirting the mountains. Deval was in no hurry. He didn't want to put too much distance between himself and the tribe in the valley. He halted the convoy at regular intervals and the men took what protection they could get from the burning sun. All except Bouchier. He would stand up in his vehicle and scan the mountains with his binoculars. They were too close to the mountains and the cover they could give the natives, for his liking. On one halt, he called Cato to him.

'Take a look at the mountains,' he ordered, and handed Cato his binoculars.

Cato studied the towering mass of rocks and scree. It wavered in the heat and made his eyes smart.

'See anything?' Bouchier asked. 'Any movement?'

'No, Sergeant.'

'They are there – somewhere,' Bouchier warned. 'They are like the Arabs of North Africa. They can hide themselves in their own dirt and sand.'

But there was no sign of anyone tailing

them all day. The men knew what Bouchier was thinking and one or two made references to the sun. Others quietly scoffed him for thinking that he was still in Algeria.

When evening came, they were half way between the valley and the coast, but still close to the foothills. Again guards were posted and fires lit. Cato and the men made themselves as comfortable as possible and relaxed in the cool of the evening. They talked amongst themselves and bedded down early, glad to have an undisturbed, peaceful night.

But again their sleep was disturbed in the early hours of the morning.

'Eee … ee! Eeee!… Eeeeeee!'

The shrill, piercing cry carried across the still night. The men awoke with a start.

'Eee!… Eeee!'

The cry made the men's nerves tingle. Then there was silence. A total, utter silence. The men felt for their rifles.

'*Sentinelle,*' Bouchier shouted. He got no response. '*Sentinelle,*' he shouted again. Again he got no response. '*Aux armes!*' he shouted. '*Aux armes!*'

The men quickly set to. It was pitch black. The fires had gone out. Cato glanced at his illuminated watch dial. It was three-thirty a.m. He should have been on guard at three, but no one had called him.

Suddenly there was a swishing sound as

something was projected through the air. The projectile landed with a gentle thud in their midst. The men flung themselves to the ground expecting an explosion, but there was none. Whatever had landed amongst them was not a grenade. Bouchier came amongst them with a torch.

'Where is it?' he growled.

'Here, Sergeant,' Greco replied.

Bouchier shone his torch. The object was a small sack, tied with a cord. The men gathered round. Cautiously, Bouchier cut the sack open. The men kept their distance. Gingerly, he turned the sack upside down and let its contents fall out. There was a gasp of surprise as the men saw a fleshy, bloody mess. It became one of horror as they recognised what it was. It was somebody's penis and testicles! Somebody had been emasculated!

'*Mon Dieu!*' Greco gasped. 'Who would do that?'

Some of them turned away. The others gripped their rifles.

'*Les cochons!*' Hook growled. 'They are inhuman!'

'The bastards!' Bouchier shouted.

'What is it, Sergeant?' Deval called out.

He came into their midst and saw the emasculated parts.

'Who is it?' he said.

Bouchier didn't answer him. He ran to his

vehicle and climbed aboard.

'Get to the ground,' he shouted. 'All of you – heads down!'

The men fell to the ground.

Bouchier uncovered his machine gun. Within seconds he was blasting away into the darkness. There was a pungent smell of spent ammunition as the night seemed to go mad with tracer bullets screaming into the distance. Bouchier sprayed the area in a circle and emptied the magazine. Then he stopped. He jumped down from the gun.

'Get rid of that,' he ordered Greco.

'Roll call, Sergeant,' Deval ordered.

'Answer your names,' Bouchier shouted. He went through the list. One man was missing – Napoleon! His tour of duty had been from one to two a.m. At two a.m. Hessler had been due to take over. He had not been called.

'Do we go after them, Sergeant?' Hook demanded.

'Where? How?' Bouchier growled. 'Which direction? Use your brains. We wait until dawn. It won't be long. Sasous, Diago – get the fires lit. We all stay awake. No one sleeps!'

There was no need to have told them. None of them could have slept after what they had seen.

Deval called Bouchier to one side.

'That is an old Moslem custom,' Bouchier growled. 'They let their woman do it.'

173

'It is not that alone that worries me,' Deval intervened.

'They got into the camp?' Bouchier asked.

'What else did they do?' Deval asked. He was worried about the success of the mission. The murder of one of his legionnaires would make the men want revenge. It would also give Deval an excuse to take any course of action that he wanted, but what else had they done? he wondered. That worried him.

'I'll start checking.'

He gave the order. The men started the search. They moved silently, and gingerly. They didn't even talk to each other. There was an uneasiness now of the hostility that surrounded them, and they were united in their feelings of hatred towards Hakim. Napoleon had been one of them. His murder appalled them. They wanted revenge.

'The radios are unserviceable,' Sasous reported. 'They have taken some of the parts.'

'Can they be repaired?' Bouchier asked.

Sasous shook his head. 'No, Sergeant.'

'*Sacre bleu!*' Bouchier growled. 'Anything else?'

Nothing came to light. The stores were still intact, so were the spare cans of petrol. It looked as if it were only the radios.

Bouchier told Deval.

'How could they do it?' Deval asked. 'How?'

'They are very clever bastards, *mon Lieutenant,*' Bouchier grunted. 'Very clever bastards.'

Bang! No sooner had Bouchier spoken than a dull explosion shattered the still night. The men flung themselves to the ground. The explosion had been short, dull and metallic.

'Watch your front!' Bouchier shouted.

'The reconnaissance car!' a voice called out.

Bang! Another dull, metallic bang made them all hug the ground again. They gripped their rifles and peered into the dark blue of the darkness. But the explosions had come from the two cars. Bouchier ran to them. Deval was already there. Somebody was lying on the ground alongside one of them.

'They've sabotaged it,' Deval said, tight lipped and angry. 'A time bomb!'

'Fetch a torch!' Bouchier shouted.

Fritz brought two torches. Bouchier got under the vehicle. It was Diago who was already on the ground.

'The rear, Sergeant,' Diago said.

Bouchier shone his torch and swore. The bomb had been well placed. The explosion had destroyed one of the most vital parts of the vehicle – the rear axle! The vehicle could not be driven! Nothing they could do would make any difference. It had been rendered useless. He scrambled out from under the vehicle and told Deval.

'The other one will be the same,' he said.

'So the reconnaissance cars are useless,' Deval gasped.

The men heard him and felt a tremor pass through their bodies. The two reconnaissance cars were immobile!

'What about the stores vehicle?' Deval asked.

There was a moment's hesitation. There had been no explosion from that vehicle, but that didn't mean that there was no charge about to explode.

'Well?' Deval demanded.

Bouchier turned to Fritz who was holding the second torch.

'Take the front,' he ordered. 'I'll inspect the rear. If you see anything – get the hell out of it!'

There was a short pause.

'Yes, Sergeant,' Fritz said.

They went to the truck and crawled under it, flashing their torches at its belly.

'Nothing,' Fritz called out from the front of the truck.

He scrambled out. Bouchier crawled under the full length of the vehicle.

'Nothing,' he reported back to Deval.

'Just the two scout cars,' Deval hissed. 'I wonder why?'

'Perhaps they hadn't time,' Bouchier

suggested, 'or perhaps they only had two charges.'

'Perhaps,' Deval muttered, but didn't sound convinced.

'We'll strip the scout cars at first light,' Bouchier said.

'Take out everything of use to them,' Deval agreed, and turned away from the Sergeant. He had lost two reconnaissance vehicles and one legionnaire, but he wasn't through. The setbacks had only hardened his determination. He was in Hakim's territory, he thought. The natives had proved that, and there had to be some reason why they had left the stores vehicle. It gave the Section a means of getting back to the *poste*. Perhaps that was what they wanted, he thought. Perhaps they didn't want the patrol in the area. Perhaps they wanted them to go back to their base.

As dawn approached, Greco made coffee. The men had little appetite for anything else. They drank their coffee and silently watched the dawn unfold before them. They felt grubby and tired, and disgusted at the thought of Napoleon's mutilated body out in the scrub. They strained their eyes expecting to see his body close by, but they saw only the scrub, the bushes, the rocks, and the barren plain. There was no sign of Napoleon. They stood on their vehicles and searched the scrubland. Then they saw a telltale sign. They saw the hovering vultures that have their own built-in radar system that homes them in on death. The men started to move forward, en mass.

'Hold it!' Bouchier shouted.

The men stood still.

'Corporal Schnell, Diago, Cato. Get a blanket and come with me. The rest of you stay where you are.'

Cato got a blanket and Bouchier led them towards the hovering vultures. They came upon Napoleon's body. It was spread-eagled – staked to the ground at the wrists and the ankles. His trousers had been ripped open and there was a pool of blood where his penis and testicles had been cut away. An army of insects were feeding on the open wound. His eyes were wide open and horror stricken. Around his mouth was a tight gag of leather. It had only been removed at the moment of incision to let his screams pierce the night. Cato felt his inside turn over.

'*Les cochons!*' Bouchier hissed. 'The bastards!'

Corporal Schnell cut the fastenings and wrapped Napoleon's body in a blanket. Cato and Diago carried him back to the camp.

The rest of the Section stood silently watching and waiting, both curious and disgusted at the pagan decimation of Napoleon's body. The body was dumped on the ground still wrapped in the blanket.

Bouchier opened it up.

'Take a good look,' he ordered. 'All of you. Take a long hard look, and remember when you are next on *sentinelle*.'

The men stood sullen. Berge went pale. But no one spoke and no one made a move. Bouchier covered the body with the blanket and reported to Lieutenant Deval.

'We can make the outpost in twenty-four hours, *mon Lieutenant*,' he said. 'They could take him to the *poste* and bury him there.'

'We bury him here, Sergeant,' Deval ordered.

The men overheard Bouchier's suggestion and were in sympathy with him. They didn't like the idea of leaving Napoleon's body on the plain. They eyed Deval sullenly. They were losing their respect for him. Diago turned his head away and spat, but Deval had his thoughts elsewhere and was oblivious to the men's resentment.

'Here,' Deval said again. 'We go back to that valley. Hakim and his men are there somewhere.'

'We could return to the outpost and radio the *poste* for a helicopter, *mon Lieutenant*,' Bouchier pointed out.

Deval's face became stern. He didn't like his orders being questioned.

'There is some reason why Hakim has left one of the trucks,' he said. 'I think he wants us to clear out of the area, or he wants to split us into two parties.' He shook his head. 'No, Sergeant. We are going to stay.' He wiped the perspiration from his brow. 'This damned heat,' he snapped. 'You had better start burying the poor creature.'

He turned his back on Bouchier as if the matter was closed. Bouchier scowled and walked back to the men. It was as Bouchier had expected. It was the way of the Legion, but there was something about the isolation of the hot, open plain that had even got under his skin. It seemed a miserable place to leave any one alone – even when they were dead.

'Hook! Boussec!' he shouted. 'Start digging a grave. Zugja, collect some stones. The rest of you start stripping the two reconnaissance cars.'

The men hesitated.

'What do you think this is?' Bouchier shouted. 'The Boy Scouts? This is the Legion and legionnaires are buried where they die. Now move it!'

The men set about their tasks.

Napoleon was buried without any ceremony. All that there was to remind the men of him was a mound of earth and stones.

'The Legion will be back to do the job properly,' Bouchier growled. He knew how the men felt.

The men continued to strip the two reconnaissance cars of anything that could be of value to Hakim's men. They worked silently, aware that they were not only going to be fighting Hakim's men, but also the heat of the sun that was beginning to burn down on them.

When they had finished, Bouchier reported to Deval.

'Seven men march,' Deval said. 'Three out front and four to the rear. Change every hour. We march south, as if making for the outpost, but we will return to their village.'

'Yes, *mon Lieutenant.*'

Bouchier detailed the first party. Diago, Irish and Hook were out in front. Cato, Greco, Zugi and Bouchier brought up the rear. The rest were in the vehicle. Deval sat alongside Corporal Schnell who was driving. The party moved off. Cato and the others gave a last look at Napoleon's grave and started marching with their heads slightly bent. No one spoke – not even those in the vehicle. The heat took away any desire for conversation.

Lieutenant Deval guided Corporal Schnell. The operation was now becoming his own personal battle. He was determined to make it his own personal victory. A success in this operation would be his springboard. He felt no remorse about Napoleon. Napoleon's mutilated body was the excuse he had needed for moving in to make contact with Hakim, just as the rifle had been his excuse to search the village. He would claim that it was a necessary act of revenge, because of the feelings of his men – because of the honour of the Legion. It was all going to work out.

As the march continued, the men came close to their breaking point. The sun was burning up their energy, and the hot wind constantly blew the sandy surface of the baked earth into their faces.

At the height of the sun's burning heat, they were in a deep wadi within two hours' march of the mouth of the valley. Deval halted the vehicle and called Bouchier to him.

'We will move in during the night,' he said. 'The men can rest.'

'They will have seen us,' Bouchier pointed out.

'Yes,' Deval agreed, 'but they will be expecting us to be making for the outpost. We'll move out just before dark in that direction. As soon as it is dark we send in two patrols. I want two natives for interrogation.'

'They will hear the truck, *mon Lieutenant.*'

'The truck will follow. It will wait until the men are in the valley.' Deval looked hard at Bouchier. 'I want two of them,' he ordered. 'I don't mind who they are.'

'Yes, *mon Lieutenant.*'

Bouchier told the men and gave his orders. Two men were posted as guards. The rest erected a canopy to protect themselves from the sun. Cato lay on the ground alongside Sasous. He was exhausted and suffering from the effects of the sun. They all were.

'I could sleep for twenty-four hours,' he sighed.

'I think *Monsieur Le Lieutenant* has other ideas,' Fritz said. 'He will not let us rest until he has captured this Hakim himself. He is too preoccupied with Hakim to even rest himself.'

Cato saw Deval studying his maps. He was filthy and unshaven like the rest of them, but he hadn't marched like the men, and Fritz was right, Deval had his mind full of Hakim.

Sasous closed his eyes.

'If there is a smile on my lips when our Sergeant calls us, just leave me here,' he said.

'Me too,' somebody added.

Cato closed his eyes, but the heat was so oppressive that he only slept fitfully.

In the early evening, before the sun had started its sharp descent, they moved out of the wadi and headed slowly south. The men had their rifles at the ready and their grenades fixed to their webbing. Greco was driving the truck. The rest of the men were split into two sections. Corporal Schnell was in charge of one, Sergeant Bouchier the other. They marched on either side of the truck about thirty metres behind it. Both Sections carried a machine gun. They were ready for any action.

Immediately the blanket of darkness enveloped them, Bouchier halted the column, and set a course for the valley. The truck remained well to their rear. An Islamic shaped moon flitted across the sky giving a faint glow, and sufficient light for the men to pick their way. They marched quickly, but rested regularly. No one spoke. They all gripped their rifle butts tightly and kept alert. They hadn't forgotten about Napoleon.

They came to the mouth of the valley and felt its silence again. But there were none of the camp fires that they had seen when they had last been in the valley, and there was no sound of any stray sheep or cattle. The valley was silent and it was deserted.

They moved, stealthily, up the valley listening for any sound of life. They came to the foot of the terraces where the natives lived in their caves.

Bouchier halted the column. The men took up a defensive position. Bouchier called Zugi to him. Zugi had changed his white robe, and looked like a black shadow in the pale moonlight.

'They have gone,' Bouchier growled. 'Over

the saddle. It must be a pass.'

'They will be close, *Sahib*. They will come back.'

'Go and tell *Monsieur Le Lieutenant*.'

Zugi doubled away. The men watched and waited. They had become adjusted to the dim light. They could see the saddle and the bushes that moved with the breeze, and they watched them closely.

Presently, they heard the stores vehicle enter the valley. The engine noise grew louder, as it came up the valley.

'That should attract the bastards,' Bouchier said, for them all to hear.

The truck came close to their position. Bouchier and Deval conferred.

'They will be curious,' Deval said. 'They will come and spy on us. They will have to come over that saddle. I want two men, Sergeant. I don't mind how you get them.'

'I will send out a party, *mon Lieutenant*. We will move the truck to the higher ground in case they attack us.'

Deval agreed. Bouchier went to the men and explained what was happening.

'The natives will be coming to watch us. We need a prisoner, even if we have to wait all night. Corporal Schnell and three men will go into the saddle. The rest of us will be on the first terrace beside the caves. We will take the truck up the track.'

There was a rough track that led to the

caves. Bouchier turned to the Corporal. 'You know what to do?'

'Yes, Sergeant.'

Bouchier grunted and went to give Greco his orders.

Schnell glanced around him. 'Hessler – Cato –Vasey,' he whispered. The men closed in on him. 'Hessler and Cato keep your rifles. Vasey get a pistol and a baton. All of you get a blanket.'

Cato and the others got their dark blankets and wrapped them over their uniforms. At a crouch they moved through the ruins of the town towards the sloping foothills that led to the saddle.

They climbed the slope quickly. Corporal Schnell was in a hurry. He darted from cover to cover. Cato and the other two followed. Just below the saddle, Schnell stopped and gathered his party around him. He pointed to four small dark mounds of rock and shrub and silently allocated one to each of them.

'Keep yourselves camouflaged,' he whispered. 'I will make the first move.' He touched Vasey on the shoulder and held up his baton. 'We go for one each.' He pointed to Cato and Hessler. 'You scare off the rest. Make a lot of noise. You, Hessler, use your grenades.'

The men moved their heads in silent agreement and moved to their positions.

Cato sat on the ground behind his rock and shrub, and covered himself with his blanket. He was almost part of the small, thorny shrub. The others had also melted into the mountain side. Beneath them was the valley. Greco had moved the truck on to the higher ground, and everything was quiet.

The minutes passed slowly. Cato gripped his rifle and wiped some of the sand away from his face. They waited for what seemed like an eternity, before they heard a faint noise. Cato froze. His pulse took off. He tried to shrink further into the bush.

There was a gentle grating noise and a figure moved down the side of the hill close to their position. Another figure passed by, and another.

Suddenly there was a sharp yell! And another! Schnell and Vasey had made their move. Cato stood up and started firing his rifle. His bullets were screeching into the darkness in the direction of the passing figures. There were two loud *bangs,* as Hessler's grenades exploded. Hessler joined in the rifle fire. They kept firing furiously. Cato turned. He saw Schnell had over-powered his man, but Vasey was locked in a tight hold. The native had a dagger in his hand. Cato quickly moved in and crashed his rifle butt into the man's head. He went sprawling to the ground.

'Thanks,' Vasey said.

'You O.K.?'

'Sure.'

Schnell came over to them. 'Pick him up,' he ordered. 'Cato, Hessler, cover us. They are around.'

Vasey lifted the body and put him over his shoulders. Schnell did the same with his. They quickly descended the slope. Cato and Hessler followed behind.

They came to their camp. Bouchier was watching for them. He didn't congratulate them. He simply growled. 'Tie them up,' and went to report to Lieutenant Deval.

Cato joined Sasous.

'Been having fun?' Sasous grinned.

Cato suddenly felt very weary.

'Go and get some coffee,' Sasous added. 'I have a feeling the night is not yet over.'

Cato went to the stores truck where Greco had prepared some coffee and food. He saw the two native prisoners. They had re-covered, but were tied and bound, and lay on the ground. Deval and Bouchier were close by. Cato heard Deval giving Bouchier his orders.

'I want to know where Hakim is and what his plans are,' he ordered, 'and why they left us one vehicle.'

'Yes, *mon Lieutenant.*'

'And, Sergeant,' Deval added, 'remember that Hakim does not take prisoners.'

There was a moment's delay before

188

Bouchier replied, 'I understand, *mon Lieu-tenant.*'

Cato gripped his mug. Vasey sidled up to him.

'That guy worries me,' he muttered.

'Get behind some cover,' Bouchier ordered. 'All of you,' he called out, 'be prepared.'

Cato joined Sasous. Bouchier got hold of Corporal Schnell.

'Take those two natives into that cave,' he ordered, indicating a nearby cave. 'Hessler and Zugja will go with you.'

He put his cane on the Corporal's arm. 'I want one of them ready to talk,' he said. He handed Schnell a long sharp knife that he had got from the stores truck. 'Remember Napoleon,' he added.

The Corporal took the knife. He went to get Hessler.

Zugi stood in the background.

Bouchier got hold of him. 'You know what the Lieutenant wants,' he growled.

Zugi's eyes opened wide.

'I know, *Sahib,*' he said.

'Then see that he gets it.'

Bouchier gave him a look of intimidation and turned away. Corporal Schnell and Hessler lifted the two natives to their feet and propelled them towards the cave. Bouchier waited a few minutes to give Schnell time to soften them up and then he joined them.

Cato and the others saw him go into the cave.

'Ee – eee – ee – e!'

A piercing scream came from the cave.

Cato froze and gripped the butt of his rifle. None of the men made any remark. They knew that Napoleon had been revenged, and they watched the dark shadows in front of them.

A sharp rifle *crack* followed the scream. Cato gritted his teeth. Deval's orders had been carried out to the letter.

Sergeant Bouchier and his party rejoined the men. Corporal Schnell and Hessler took up a position in the group. They spoke to no one and nothing was said. Zugi sat trembling behind his cover.

'Hakim and his men are in the mountains,' Bouchier told Deval. 'He intends to attack the outpost and then the *poste*, but he is waiting for a supply caravan that is coming from the coast.'

'Very good, Sergeant,' Deval said. 'Very good. And they left us the truck so that we would return to the outpost.'

'Yes, *mon Lieutenant*.'

Deval could see it all quite clearly. Their reconnaissance to the coast would have intercepted the caravan, and Hakim needed the supplies before he could make his move.

'The two natives were part of a patrol sent out to meet the caravan,' Bouchier said.

'There is a pass over the saddle into Hakim's camp.'

'If we can stop the supplies reaching Hakim, Sergeant, then we can stop Hakim.'

'They know we are here,' Bouchier warned.

'Then we must be prepared for anything. See to it.'

Bouchier went around the men and told them about the supplies caravan and warned them not to relax their vigil. Deval took up his own position and waited. He was well pleased with the turn of events. He felt an excitement that he had never felt before. He sensed the sweet smell of success and its narcosis gripped him. He had never felt such elation before.

But suddenly his taste of success turned sour. A faint red glow appeared in the sky at the mouth of the valley. Deval saw it as Bouchier reported it.

'It could be a direction signal, *mon Lieutenant,*'he suggested.

Deval knew otherwise. His face clouded over.

'They don't need any direction signals,' he snapped. 'They have been warned.'

His feeling of excitement had turned to annoyance.

'Damn!' he hissed. 'Damn!'

Suddenly there were a series of rifle cracks and bullets started whining off the rocks around their position.

'*Aux armes!*' Bouchier shouted. He left Deval and went around the men. The rifle shots had ceased.

'Try and locate their positions,' he hissed, 'and then give them hell.'

Suddenly a large flaming bomb came hurtling through the air. It exploded close to the truck.

The men started firing in the direction from which it had come. More bullets started to smack into the rocks around the men. Somebody gave a yell of pain. Two more flame bombs came at them. Again they fell short. The men blasted away at everything and nothing – firing wild. A bomb exploded near the truck. The vehicle canopy caught fire. It started to spread and burn like paper.

'Take cover!' Bouchier yelled. 'Take cover!'

The flames had spread. The canopy was fully ablaze and so was the camouflage netting. A figure suddenly emerged from behind some rocks and darted across to the truck. He climbed into the driver's cab. The vehicle lurched forward. It started to roll down the incline. It gathered momentum. The figure jumped clear. The men hugged the ground. The truck hit a boulder and lurched on to its side. There was a sheet of flame and a tremendous explosion that sent a blast wave across the valley. In seconds the truck had been reduced to a burning mass of rubble. The men got up from the ground. The shooting had died away. The only sound was the crackle of flames as the vehicle burned. Bouchier went around the men and moved them to form a protective ring around their encampment.

'Fire at anything that moves, or makes a noise,' he hissed. 'If anybody gets past you, I'll kill you myself.'

It had been Greco who had moved the vehicle, but he had been caught by the explosion. His uniform was torn and his right arm burned. Boussec had also got a flesh wound in the arm during the shooting.

Diago crawled over to where Greco was lying. Fritz was bandaging his arm.

'You O.K.?' Diago asked.

Greco indicated his bandaged arm. 'Except for this.'

'Hurt much?'

'Some. Pity we lost the truck.'

'We could have all been killed,' Diago said. 'You did a good job, *mon brave.*'

He turned and crawled back to his position. There had always been an undercurrent of feeling between the two men, but not any longer. Fritz gave a faint smile and continued bandaging Greco's arm.

Bouchier examined what stores remained.

'We still have plenty of ammunition, *mon Lieutenant,*' he reported. 'Also water and some of the hard tack.'

But the men had lost their bedrolls and there were no fires. The cold, night air had got through their extra garments and chilled their bodies. A dejected silence settled over the area.

Cato lay behind his wall and stared into the darkness. Several metres to his right was Sasous. To his left was Hook. No one spoke. They all lay and listened. For a while Cato reflected on his change of circumstances. A few days earlier he had been fully concerned with Pedrides. It had been paramount in his mind. Now it was secondary. All that mattered for him now was survival.

Deval also reflected on his sudden change of fortune. He sat, tight lipped and stern, and waited impatiently for the dawn.

With the dawn came a flood of emotions from the men – relief, concern, anxiety and disillusionment. It was another day and they had survived the night. But they were without any transport, or radio, and they had very little food. They had had little sleep over the past three nights and the sun during the day had taken its toll. They were tired and weary, and they were two days' march away from the outpost. Cato saw their plight reflected in the men's eyes and on their grubby faces that showed several days' growth of beard and was covered with yellow dust. He also saw the look on the faces of Corporal Schnell and Hessler. Schnell's face looked stark and sad. His role in the torture of the prisoners was apparently troubling him deeply. Hessler also had a guilty look about him.

Greco and Fritz were able to prepare some coffee. The men gladly accepted it and retreated to their cover.

Bouchier soon made himself heard. His manner and attitude hadn't changed since their first meeting. He still wore his gloves and always had his cane close at hand. His features looked even more aggressive with his beard and the effects of the sun and sand, but he was still Sergeant Bouchier of the French Foreign Legion and he gave no quarter. Only the men had less fear of him now. Even Boussec who had always jumped and sweated at Bouchier's bark, returned his caustic comments with a look of sullen defiance. Bouchier was having an uphill battle. The men were losing confidence in their leader, and in the outcome of their fight against the natives. Bouchier knew how they felt about the Lieutenant and it made him even more blistering in his attacks on them.

'Hakim's stores caravan will now be making for the outpost,' Deval told Bouchier. 'That is the only other pass into Hakim's territory and that ties in with his plans. My guess is that he will be joining the caravan at that pass. If we move quickly we can get there before him and trap him and his caravan in a cross fire.'

'Hakim will already have made his move for the outpost, *mon Lieutenant*,' Bouchier pointed out. 'He has a start on us.'

'The outpost is two days' march away. He has to use the mountains as cover. We can use the plains and move faster. Besides, Hakim will have to rest before he makes his attack.'

'Our men are tired and weary, *mon Lieutenant*,' Bouchier warned.

Deval cast that aside.

'They are legionnaires,' he snapped, 'and in the Legion they march or die. They have the alternative.'

Deval's tone gave no quarter for discussion. The look on his face told Bouchier that there was no room for flexibility. Deval had his eyes now set on making physical contact with Hakim. The determination would drive him to any limits of physical endurance and the men were going to have to go along with him – or die!

'We travel light,' Deval ordered. 'Machine guns, ammunition, weapons and water. Distribute the hard rations, but the men will only eat and drink when ordered. Zugja will leave immediately. He can move much quicker than us. He can warn the outpost.'

Deval turned his attention to the maps, and Bouchier rejoined the men.

Bouchier gave Zugi his orders. Zugi accepted them gladly.

He bid a quick farewell to the men and set off at the double. Cato and the men silently watched him, until Bouchier turned on them.

'We march or die!' he shouted. 'You joined the Legion to march. Now we march! And we travel light.'

He snapped out his orders. The men truculently obeyed. They were sluggish and slow.

'*Pronto!*' Bouchier shouted, 'before Hakim's men pick you off, or the sun burns you up.'

THIRTEEN

The men marched slowly along the valley and kept casting furtive glances at the mountain sides. They were weary, and suspicious of Hakim's men. They had been surprised by them twice. It could happen again. Only Corporal Schnell seemed unconcerned. He was about fifty metres in front of the column and he moved at a trot, as if his eyes were fixed, rigidly, on the horizon ahead of him.

They came to the neck of the valley and the men walked with even more caution. It was the ideal place for an ambush.

Sergeant Bouchier went up to Deval.

'They could be waiting for us,' he warned.

Deval withdrew his binoculars and scanned the valley. 'There is nobody there,' he said.

The men also saw nothing suspicious, but they still held back. Deval, irritably, urged them on, but the men were not enthusiastic. Corporal Schnell stopped and looked back for orders. He had almost reached the outlet and was approaching a small cluster of large, prickly bushes and stilted trees. Deval moved his arm urging him to increase his pace. Schnell started to trot again. The men trudged cautiously forward.

'Ee ... ee!'

Schnell gave out a short, agonising cry that re-echoed around the valley. Cato froze as the cry lingered. He could see Corporal Schnell in an upright position with his head sagged forward.

'*Merde!*' someone hissed. 'Booby trap!'

Booby trap! Cato looked again at Schnell. He was still in an upright position, but his whole body had now sagged. He looked like a lifeless puppet that was being held upright by hidden strings. The men looked away. They knew that their Corporal Schnell was dead!

'Watch your fronts!' Bouchier shouted.

The men readily responded and took up positions to protect their position. Nothing happened. The valley was silent again. One by one they cast furtive glances back at Schnell. He hadn't moved.

'Hessler! Hook!'

Bouchier called out the two men's names. He waved his arm telling them to follow him. Hook hesitated. Hessler followed without delay.

'Come on, Hook,' Bouchier hissed.

Hook moved slowly and joined the other two. They kept their eyes pinned to the ground and picked their way forward. Deval waited with increasing impatience. He knew that a delay could be serious. If they were to be of any help to the outpost, there had to be no stoppages.

Schnell was dead – pinned to a thin, upright, bamboo cane by a short, steel dagger attached to the top of the cane. The dagger had pierced his chest. His eyes and mouth were wide open. Bouchier withdrew his hatchet knife and cut him loose. He fell to the ground. Hessler stared at Schnell's still form with a look of disbelief on his face. Bouchier examined the booby trap. It was simple and effective. The bamboo cane had been set deep in the ground and pulled behind a tree stump and held so that it would act like the recoil of a spring on release. A simple trip cord had released its fastenings. It had whip-lashed into Schnell's chest. Bouchier scowled. 'Somebody is teaching the bastards fancy tricks,' he growled. 'It was well camouflaged.'

He hacked his long knife at the bushes for any further signs of traps, but found none. He returned to Hook and Hessler.

'Don't just look at him,' he snapped. 'He's dead. Take him back.'

The two men lifted the body gingerly and carried it back to the section. The others learned the worst. They watched Hook and Hessler lay Schnell's body on the ground with the end of the dagger still in his body, and were stunned. It seemed unbelievable that Schnell should be killed by a booby trap. Schnell of all people.

'Schnell, a booby trap!' Irish hissed, voicing their surprise.

Schnell had been the ideal legionnaire and he had seen it all before. But Cato recalled the sad look in Schnell's eyes and the way he had moved up the valley as if his thoughts had been far away. Schnell hadn't been thinking of booby traps, he thought. Schnell had had other things on his mind!

'A simple booby trap,' Bouchier told Deval, and explained its operation. 'They used something similar in Indo-China,' he added.

Deval's face looked stern. He wasn't interested in the history, or the technicalities, of the booby trap. The delay was annoying him.

'Bury him at the foot of the mountains,' he ordered, 'and be quick.'

Bouchier gave his orders. The men moved gingerly to the foot of the slopes and again took up a defensive position. Some of them gathered rocks. They had no time to dig a grave. Bouchier emptied the Corporal's pockets.

The men whispered amongst themselves.

'*Mon Dieu!* They are picking us off one by one.'

'They could have the whole valley booby trapped.'

'We should go over the mountains.'

'What do you think, Cato?' Diago asked. 'Will *The Snake* do that?'

'Time is against us,' Cato whispered. 'He'll make us go through the valley, and keep to the plain.'

'The plain will be hell,' Irish growled.

They finished covering Schnell's body, but they were reluctant to move off.

'The neck of the valley will all be booby trapped,' Diago said, voicing their fears.

'We should keep close to the side of the mountains,' someone called out.

'We move out!' Bouchier ordered. 'Or else…' He moved his rifle along the group of men.

'Which way, Sergeant?' Diago asked.

'You know which way, Diago – the quickest way! Across the plain.'

'We'll all die on the plain,' Greco said.

Bouchier's face became inflamed, but before his fury burst, Deval was in their midst. He had stood aside while the men had buried Schnell. He had been studying the neck of the valley with his binoculars. He had appeared pre-occupied, but he had heard the men grumbling. He had heard their whispers and suggestions. He knew how they felt and he was both contemptuous of them, and angry. He was contemptuous of their logic in preferring to cross the mountains than the plain. He knew that the mountains provided cover for Hakim's men, who could pick them off one by one. On the plain they would be safe, unless Hakim's men attacked outright, which was unlikely. But he knew that the men feared the isolation and heat of the plain, and this made him angry, because their fear of the plain would slow them down, and that was something he couldn't allow. The only chance he had to salvage any glory out of the situation was to get to the outpost before Hakim. He had lost his vehicles and some of his men. He had to justify his actions. He had to safeguard his future. He had to get to the outpost as soon as possible and if some of the men died on the way, that was just too bad.

'All of you!' he snapped. 'All of you, listen to me.'

The men immediately stopped what they were doing and looked at him. His tone had demanded immediate attention and he got it. He stood with his feet apart and his hands on his hips. His face was bearded and grubby like the men's, but his lips were tightly pressed together and his eyes flashed, angrily, from man to man. He meant business. Cato saw the wild look in his eyes and knew that he had lost his composure.

'I've heard all your whispers and your grumbles,' Deval sneered. 'You are like a pack of school girls. You don't deserve to call yourself legionnaires.'

Some of them looked at him defiantly, others looked away, but they were all used to being derided by Bouchier. Deval's scorn had little effect.

'It will take us less than two days' march to reach the outpost,' Deval said, 'and we are going to do just that, because if we don't, we won't reach the outpost in time to stop Hakim's men.' He eyed them all. 'There won't even be an outpost!' he snapped. 'So we are going to march out of this valley and we are going to march out quickly.'

'It is booby trapped,' Hook growled.

Deval was taken aback by the statement. He had not expected any opposition.

'Be quiet,' Bouchier snarled, but Hook's remark had given the others confidence.

'We have better cover in the mountains,' Irish said.

'Don't be so stupid!' Deval shouted. 'You are safer on the plain than in the mountains.'

'They could pick us off on the plain,' someone called out. 'Just like they did Napoleon.'

'We will all die in any case,' Diago growled.

'Silence!' Deval roared. 'Silence!'

His face looked like thunder. That the men should question his orders had ignited the fuse that released his wrath and contempt of them. It exploded like a bomb.

'You dare to question my orders!' he shouted. 'You actually dare!' He eyed them

204

one by one with his mouth twisted in a mocking smile.

'So you worry in case you might die,' he sneered.

There was a look in his eyes that told Cato there was a lot more to come. It also told him that Deval couldn't stop it coming. He had opened the flood gates. He was about to blow his top.

'If the truth was known,' he shouted, 'you probably all deserve to die!'

Cato looked at him aghast. Even Sergeant Bouchier looked taken aback by the blunt, callous outburst of contempt. It was not expected from an officer.

'So you are concerned that you might die?' Deval mocked again. 'And what about the people you have already destroyed? What about the deeds that brought you all scurrying into the Legion for protection?'

No one answered him, but his question had hit home. One or two of them looked away.

'You, legionnaire?' he asked Fritz. 'Why do you hate yourself so much? Why did you leave your comrades?'

Fritz dropped his eyes and looked away. It gave Deval encouragement. He turned on Greco.

'And you?' he shouted. 'Were you really the great revolutionary? Your country has changed its ways. Why are you with us? Why do you hide from your own people – or did you turn and run?' His face twisted into a look of scorn. Greco's face had paled. Deval's wild guess had been near the mark. He turned on Cato and gave a look of derision.

'Ah! *Le Legionnaire Cato*,' he said. 'The knight in shining armour. The man out for revenge.'

Cato stood his ground.

'Bah!' Deval snapped. 'You found your man and what did you do? Nothing! Absolutely nothing!'

Cato's face muscles went taut and he clenched his fist. Deval was sick, but he was opening up an old wound, and it hurt. He turned his back on him.

'You disgust me,' Deval snarled. He turned on Diago. He had got the bit between his teeth. He was enjoying himself.

'*Le Legionnaire Diago*,' he mocked. 'The man who hates the fascists who run his country. Is that really the case? Or was it not the reverse? Was it not that the people hated you? Were you not one of the fascists yourself?'

Diago turned his head away and spat, but he didn't deny Deval's accusation. Deval gave a scornful laugh. He turned on Irish. Irish looked away.

'And how many people are on your conscience?' Deval shouted.

Irish's shoulders sagged and his face

looked pained. Deval turned away from him and looked at Hessler.

'Ah, *Le Legionnaire Hessler*,' he said. 'The man who never closes his eyes.' He gave a snarl of disgust. 'Tell us why?'

Hessler's eyes became inflamed. He brought his rifle barrel to point at Deval. 'You wouldn't do that,' Deval mocked. 'Not you. You are too well disciplined. Put it down!'

Hessler hesitated, momentarily, and then lowered his rifle.

'*Mon Dieu*,' Deval hissed. 'It must have been some filthy deed to keep you awake every night. You poor miserable creature.'

He turned away from him in disgust. There was a pregnant silence. The men were all rooted to where they stood. Those that Deval had degraded heard his words through a mist. They registered, but made no deep impression. Those who he was yet to castigate were already examining their own misdeeds.

Deval turned to where Hook, Boussec and Vasey stood together.

'Now here we have two killers,' he derided. He looked at Vasey. 'Or is it three?' he asked. 'What brought you from the gutters of New York? Another killing?'

'One more would make little difference, *Lootenant*,' Vasey growled in his broad American accent, and raised the barrel of his rifle, menacingly.

'You will regret that remark, legionnaire,' Deval shouted. A look of satisfaction appeared on his face. 'When we get back to the *poste* you will be punished. Bah!' He spat on the ground and turned on Berge. Berge dropped his eyes. Deval hesitated. He knew about Berge. Sergeant Bouchier caught the hesitation and the look of uncertainty in the Lieutenant's eyes.

'And what about you?' Deval asked finally. 'Was it the cheating, or the lying, or just the disgrace that killed your father?'

Berge turned his back on him. Deval breathed heavily and turned on Sasous. Sasous he also knew about.

'And you?' he sneered. 'What about you?'

'Yes, *mon Lieutenant?*' Sasous asked. 'What about me?'

'You're finished, Sasous,' Deval scoffed. 'You can't be trusted by your own scum.' He gave a mocking laugh. 'You – the pride of the underworld; the king of the prostitutes and pimps, but not any longer, and no wonder. You let your friends die because you were too busy enjoying yourself with some cheap harlot!'

Sasous calmly withdrew a cigarette from his pocket and lit it.

'She was a real woman, *mon Lieutenant,*' he said, 'but you wouldn't know about women.'

Deval's face flushed up. He clenched his fists again.

'What do you mean?' he shouted.

Sasous smoked his cigarette.

'You know what I mean, *mon Lieutenant*. I am talking about women!'

Deval's face looked as if he was about to explode. It was white with rage.

'You'll regret that,' he thundered. 'You'll regret that. You'll see. You'll regret that.' But he turned away from Sasous.

'All of you,' he shouted. 'All of you...' He was momentarily lost for words. 'All of you – we go after Hakim, and we go across the plain or you stay here and die. You are legionnaires, and you will fight like legionnaires.' He turned to Bouchier. 'Get these men ready to move out, or they die here,' he barked, and walked away from them all.

There was a moment's uncertainty. Bouchier had never heard such an outburst. He went quickly into action before they had time to react.

'Move it! Move it!' he shouted. 'Get ready to move out. Pronto! Pronto!'

There was no hesitation. The men had no unity to disobey. They were all with their own problems. They started to collect their gear together, but they moved with their heads bent and eyes averted from each other. They were like naked men, embarrassed to look at each other.

Bouchier went up to Deval. Deval's lips were still tightly pressed together and his eyes alert and flashing.

'We will have no more trouble,' Deval said. 'They will behave like legionnaires now.'

'Yes, *mon Lieutenant*,' Bouchier agreed, and held his ground. 'You left one man out, *mon Lieutenant*,' he added.

Deval looked at him. Their eyes met. Bouchier eyes didn't flinch. His face was hard set.

'You bared all their souls,' he said. 'Could you also bare mine?'

'I could,' Deval agreed, 'but I need your support.'

'You will still get it, *mon Lieutenant*.'

Deval caught the determination in Bouchier's voice and the stubbornness in his eyes.

'All right, Sergeant,' he said. Again a glint appeared in his eyes as if he was enjoying himself. 'You are one of the old school – a tough bully. A man who sticks to the rules. The men loath you and your fellow *sous officers* suffer you. But you get results and that's all that matters as far as I am concerned.'

'And do I also deserve to die?'

'I think you would welcome death, Sergeant,' Deval mused, 'because you are really a very lonely man.' He shook his head, sadly. 'Very lonely. You have no one. You love no one and no one loves you.'

'Do you also want to die, *mon Lieutenant?*'

he asked.

'No, I do not,' Deval snapped, 'and I don't intend to if I can help it. Nobody will die if everyone obeys my orders.'

His face clouded over. He had tired of the discussion. 'Get the men moving,' he ordered. 'We want no more delays.'

Bouchier still held his ground.

'You are wrong on one account, *mon Lieutenant*,' he said. 'I do have something.'

'And what is that?'

Bouchier shook his head. 'I wouldn't give you that pleasure, *mon Lieutenant*,' he said, and walked back to the men.

'Get your *képis* on,' he shouted. 'You are legionnaires and you'll behave like legionnaires. Get that pack on your back, Diago – Irish!'

'Yes, Sergeant?'

'You will go forward with Cato. Hook! You and Hessler bring up the rear. All of you.' The men looked at him. 'Don't you let me down,' he snarled, 'or else…'

The men quickly responded. They readily exchanged their bush hats for their white hats, and moved out without further delay.

They found two booby traps in the neck of the valley, similar to the one that had killed Corporal Schnell. Bouchier released the springs with his hatchet knife and the daggers whipped into the vertical killing position. But

211

Bouchier didn't give the men time to dwell on the traps. He kept them on the move. They soon came to the river wadi that meandered its way into the plain and were free of the valley. But they did not feel free from danger. The mountains were still close at hand, and Bouchier's constant glances in their direction reminded them of the last time he had felt that someone was trailing them. By mid-morning, they also had the heat and physical exhaustion to contend with. The sun was blazing down at them from a cloudless sky. It had already parched and baked the plain. It was doing the same to them. Their mouths and throats were arid dry and dusty. They longed to use their water bottles, but they were under strict orders only to drink when they were told to, and then only to drink small quantities. The heat tired them physically and they laboured with every step, but Deval was in a hurry. He drove them on, his only concession was to take them closer to the foot of the mountains. There was a greater risk of being sniped at by Hakim's scouts, but there was also the large boulders and projection outcrops that offered shade and relief from the sun, when they halted. Neither Cato and Sasous, or any of the others, spoke to each other at these halts, but there was no longer any embarrassment amongst them over Deval's outburst. That had been forgotten. All that mattered was to keep up with each other and get to the outpost.

But in mid-afternoon they suffered another casualty.

Deval had kept them marching on a bearing that was the most direct route, but he had kept sufficient distance between the column and the mountains to prevent a sniping attack. When he had called a halt he had been prepared to risk the danger for the cover offered by the mountain slopes, but they had always taken precautions.

In the mid afternoon, they faced a spur that projected into the plain. Deval hesitated. He scanned the mountain slopes with his binoculars and saw nothing suspicious. Bouchier came up to him. Silently, Deval handed him the binoculars. Bouchier also saw nothing suspicious.

'But I can feel them,' he growled.

Deval looked at the desert plain. The heat haze shimmered in front of his eyes. He wiped away the grime from his face and parched lips. It would have to be a wide detour to avert the spur, he thought, and it would take time. He replaced his binoculars in their case and decided to take the short route. He set a course that would pass close to the point of the spur. Bouchier returned to his position in the line. The men trudged wearily forward. They had forgotten about Hakim's scouts and what they could do.

They snaked their way over the baked earth, avoiding the gorse bushes, and constantly wiping away the sand that was being blown into their faces. They came close to the mountains and sensed a slight drop in temperature.

Crack!

One solitary shot rang out! The men immediately fell to the ground. Bouchier's eyes danced over the rocks. He saw nothing. He swore. So did the men. Then they heard a cry. They looked along the line.

'It is Diago!' someone hissed. 'He's been hit!'

Diago! Shot!

Deval heard the news and silently cursed. He ordered Bouchier to investigate. Bouchier crawled along the line.

'Keep your eyes on those rocks,' he ordered, as he passed the men. 'The bastard is up there somewhere.'

He came to Diago. He was lying on his back. Fritz was protecting him from the sun. Bouchier crawled up to them.

'How bad is it?' he asked.

Diago half sat up. His face was covered with yellow dust from his fall on the ground. There was a trickle of blood from his mouth.

'I'm O.K., Sergeant,' he said, with difficulty.

'Lie back,' Fritz said.

He put a pack under Diago's head and

sheltered him from the sun.

'Where is it?' Bouchier asked.

'In the back,' Diago coughed. 'I'll be O.K.'

Bouchier looked at Fritz. Fritz shook his head, sadly.

'How does it look?' Diago asked.

'There is very little bleeding,' Fritz said. 'I will put on a field dressing.'

Bouchier and Fritz exchanged glances again. They knew that the bleeding would be internal.

Brrr ... brrrr ... brr.

A sudden burst from one of their machine guns made them drop their heads.

The firing stopped.

'I've got him!' Vasey shouted. 'I got the bastard.'

'Keep down!' Bouchier yelled. 'Keep down! There may be more.'

He turned to Fritz. 'Stay with him,' he ordered, and crawled back to Deval, who was studying the mountains with his binoculars.

'We got one of them,' Deval said, 'but there are probably more.'

'Diago's been hit,' Bouchier reported.

'Bad?' Deval asked, still scanning the mountains.

'Yes, very bad. In the back.'

Deval lowered his binoculars. For a moment he said nothing, then he turned to Bouchier.

'Can we carry him?'

'He wouldn't last the journey.'

'He'll die if we leave him here.'

'If we get to the outpost, we can radio for a helicopter. That would give him, at least, a better chance than carrying him.'

Deval turned away and picked up his binoculars again. He liked the Sergeant's suggestion. It would put new life into the men, he thought. It would urge them on, and that suited his purpose.

'We'll do that,' he agreed. 'Let the men know. We will try to make better time. We can get clear of this range if we move quickly.'

Bouchier crawled back along the line. He collected two water bottles on the way and told them what was intended. Fritz was still with Diago. There was another trickle of blood at Diago's mouth.

'Listen to me, Diago,' Bouchier said. He looked Diago straight in the eye. 'We are going to make a shelter for you and leave you here.'

Diago's eyes opened wide.

'If we hurry we can get to the outpost by the morning,' Bouchier explained, 'and we can radio for a helicopter to come for you straight away. Otherwise we carry you, and it will take twice as long to get to the *poste,* and you must remain still.'

'But I can walk, Sergeant,' Diago pleaded.

'O.K. Diago,' Boucher said. 'You walk!'

216

He looked at Fritz. 'Let him walk!'

Fritz hesitated and moved away. The sun blazed down on the stricken Diago. He twisted his body to one side and put his arms on the ground. He tried to lift himself. He coughed and fell back. Fritz wiped the blood from his mouth and his brow.

'Yes, Sergeant,' Diago said. 'You win.'

Bouchier looked about him. He saw a large crater nearby with several bushes in it.

'Help me carry him over there,' he said to Fritz, indicating the crater.

They lifted Diago, carefully, and carried him to the new position. The others in the section watched from their firing position. They felt sorry for Diago. Deval's earlier exposure of Diago's past meant nothing to them. Diago was one of them, and he was now lying with a bullet hole in his guts.

Bouchier and Fritz laid Diago close to a bush. They gathered some bushes and were able to give Diago some protection from the sun.

'I would like to remain with him,' Fritz said, when they had finished.

'We need every man,' Bouchier growled.

'I'm staying, Sergeant,' Fritz said.

Bouchier looked at him, aggressively.

'For God's sake!' Fritz fumed. 'You can't leave anybody out here by themselves. Somebody has to stay with him.'

Bouchier looked as if he was going to

217

argue the point, and then decided other-wise.

'O.K.,' he growled. 'You stay!'

He placed the two extra water containers on the ground alongside Diago.

'Thanks, Sergeant,' Fritz said.

'Don't thank me,' Bouchier snapped. He moved away and ran back to where Deval was waiting.

'Fritz is staying with him,' he reported. He knew Deval would protest so he added quickly, 'Diago could be dead before the night is out.'

'They both could be,' Deval snorted.

'No man should die alone out here, *mon Lieutenant*,' Bouchier added.

Deval didn't reply. He got up from the ground and ran, at a crouch, to where Diago was lying. He saw the situation and the blood on Diago's lips.

'We'll get a helicopter to you as soon as possible,' he said. 'Have you sufficient water and ammunition?'

'Yes,' Fritz replied, and added flatly, *'mon Lieutenant.'*

Deval found himself lost for words. Fritz had turned his back on him. Diago looked at him and gave him no encouragement.

'We'll get help to you,' Deval said, and moved away.

Another figure came weaving to their position. It was Cato. He crouched down beside

Diago. Without saying anything, he took his hand. Diago gave a faint smile.

'We won't forget,' Cato said. He turned to Fritz. 'We'll get to the outpost as quickly as possible, *mon ami.*'

'Thanks, Cato– *Au revoir.*'

Cato looked into Fritz's face. Fritz's two days growth of beard was dirty and untidy, but his eyes were clear and true. They looked at Cato and Cato saw that Fritz was happy to stay and help Diago to die in peace.

'Take care, Cato,' Diago coughed.

'I'll tell you all about it,' Cato replied.

He ran back to his position in the line.

Deval gave the order to move out. They moved quickly, darting across the ground so as not to present an easy target. But there were no more shots. It had been a solitary sniper and a solitary shot. One shot and now the sniper was dead, and Diago was dying.

But Diago was tough. He wasn't going to die without a fight. He lay on the ground and fought grimly to live. Fritz sat with him. They spoke little to each other during the burning heat of the day. Occasionally Diago would cough up some blood and Fritz would wipe his mouth and give him a small amount of water. Fritz also kept a watch for Hakim's men, but he saw no one and heard nothing. The horizon of the plain danced in front of his eyes, and behind him the mountains seemed deserted. Later, Diago closed his eyes and slept fitfully with a fever that made him mutter incoherent words in his native tongue. In the early part of the evening, when the burning heat gave way to a more bearable temperature, he awoke. His eyes looked sunken and his body weakened.

'You should have gone with the rest,' he grumbled.

Fritz shook his head. 'And left you? No, *mon ami.*'

'You might die as well.'

Again he coughed.

'We all die some day,' Fritz smiled. 'That is the only thing certain in this life. It is only a speck of time that we wait.'

'Don't you fear death?' Diago asked.

'I do not fear it, but I do not think about it,' Fritz replied. 'It is inevitable.'

He moved away from Diago and looked at the mountains again. He had watched them during the long afternoon without seeing anyone, but this time it was different. There were two native warriors on the slopes in front of them. He slipped further behind their cover and watched them closely. The two natives were standing over the dead body of their scout, attracted to it by the vultures. They turned and waved their rifles to the south. Then they turned their attention to the plain. Fritz crept further under his cover and lay hidden. When he looked up again the two warriors were running along the side of the mountain, away from the body, like two mountain goats. He crept back to Diago. It was turning dusk. Soon the darkness would envelop them. It might also protect them.

'Fritz!' Diago called out.

Fritz turned to him. In the dimming light of the moon, Diago had taken on a grotesque look. His eyes were sunken and glazed. He was sinking fast.

'If they come during the night?' Diago asked, in between bouts of coughing.

'We will be ready for them.'

Fritz moved back. Diago raised his arm to try and hold him, but his arm fell to his side again.

'What is it?' Fritz asked.

'What the Lieutenant said about me was true,' Diago half whispered.

'Don't talk about it,' Fritz pleaded.

'Please let me,' Diago said. 'I am a Catholic, Fritz. Let me confess.'

Fritz listened to the night sounds and heard something. He got his rifle and kept it in his hands.

'You tell me,' he whispered. 'You talk as much as you like.'

There was somebody out there, he thought. Diago should remain silent, but Diago was dying and he had a right to confess his sins.

'My mother could not provide for our family,' Diago whispered with difficulty. 'She used to do without. We were starving. It isn't right that people should live like that. It makes you feel dirty.' He coughed up some more blood. Fritz wiped it away. 'I wanted to help my mother and my family. The only way I knew how was to become a servant of the Fascist Party. I was their spy.' He closed his eyes and remained silent for a while. 'I helped my family, but the people hated me, and I hated myself. I fell in love with a girl. Her name was Rossena. She returned my love, but her family would have nothing to do with me. We met secretly and one night we made love. It was not rape, but her family called it rape.' He swallowed some saliva. 'I loved her, Fritz. She loved me.'

Fritz wiped his brow.

'I understand,' he said. 'God will also understand.'

'God? Do you believe in God?' Diago asked.

'Yes,' Fritz replied. 'I do.'

'But you are a...'

'I was a Communist, yes,' Fritz intervened. 'My father was also a Minister of the Lutheran Church. I didn't believe, but I do now.' He looked away at the starlit night.

'Tell me about it, Fritz,' Diago pleaded.

'My mother and brothers were killed in

the war,' Fritz said in a whisper. 'Our home and our town were destroyed. I couldn't reconcile that with my religion, so I turned away from God. I worked for the Communists. I believed in their cause, until I saw how cruel and greedy they could be. They were no better than the Fascists who had brought our people to their ruin.'

He looked at Diago. Diago's eyes were fixed upon him in a strange glaze.

'I was running a factory,' Fritz said. 'My masters wanted a list of workers who were the least essential. They claimed that the factory was over-staffed. Some of the workers were to be made redundant and offered other employment. I had to make out that list. All the people on the list were shipped off to Siberia.' He sighed. 'They had become second class citizens.' He gripped his rifle and looked into the darkness. 'It was inhuman.'

'And now you believe in God?' Diago said. 'You believe in God.'

A faint smile had appeared on his lips. Fritz saw it in the dull light and knew that Diago was gaining strength from Fritz's admission of faith.

'Not because of that,' Fritz said. 'That just made me ashamed of myself. There are many reasons why I believe. I would have joined the Church, but that would have been too easy. I had to find my self respect again first.'

'You are a good man, Fritz,' Diago whispered.

'No, I am just a man like you, Diago, who wants to be good. Just as you did.'

Diago started coughing again. Fritz eased him into a more comfortable position so that the blood he coughed up would not choke him. When he had stopped coughing, Fritz listened again to the murmuring of the breeze through the bushes. He heard a strange noise and gripped his rifle. They were closing in on them, he thought. A sudden yell made him start.

Swish! A dagger came through the air and landed close to Diago's body. Instantly Fritz fired his rifle. He fired again and again. He was firing blind into the darkness in the direction from which the dagger had been thrown. He got up from his position and darted to another bush, and fired to the rear of their position. He could see no one, but he kept blasting away. When his gun was empty, he quickly reloaded and darted to another position and started firing again. He didn't know what he was firing at, but he kept darting to different sides of the crater and firing into the darkness. After he had emptied his gun for the third time and reloaded, he unclipped his two grenades from his chest webbing. He pulled a pin with his teeth and threw the grenade. There was a loud explosion and then silence. He kept the other in his hand and crawled back to Diago.

Diago hadn't moved. He still lay where he had lain all day – but Diago would never move again. He was dead! Somehow Hakim's men had got to him. There was a dagger sticking out of his chest!

'Oh, no!' Fritz groaned. 'Oh, no!'

He felt the full force of a great personal loss. He felt it deep in the pit of his stomach. It made him heave and left him feeling very weak. In the distance, he heard a native voice call out. He sat alongside the dead Diago with his rifle by his side and a grenade in his hand. But he had little fight left in him, or desire to kill.

FOURTEEN

Cato and the others marched themselves into the ground. Not because of Deval's urging, or the thought of outsmarting Hakim and getting revenge, but because of Diago and Fritz. The sooner the men got to the outpost, the sooner help could be sent to Diago and Fritz, and that had become very important. There had developed a genuine comradeship for one another.

When Deval finally called a halt, it was late into the night, and they were in striking distance of the outpost. They would reach it early the following day.

They sat on the ground and wet their swollen mouths. Sasous put his hand on Cato's shoulder and gave a long, meaningful sigh. They were all equally spent. They spoke little to each other. Bouchier detailed his guards and gave his orders with less vehemence than he had done in the past. Again there were no fires lit for fear of giving away their position. They huddled together for warmth as the temperature rapidly dropped, and the cold breeze swirled over their heads. Greco produced a small bottle of brandy which he silently passed around. The men took a drink and passed it on. Deval tactfully kept his distance. If he felt the cold, he gave no indication of it, and the men felt no concern for him at all. Irish and Vasey were posted on *sentinelle*. The others scratched out shallow pits in the soft, loose sand and covered their bodies with the sand for extra warmth. As the strange insect sounds of the night, and the cold, enveloped them, they lay back and closed their eyes. Cato thought back to Deval's outburst, but put it to one side. Instead, he thought of Diago and Fritz. He remembered the time that Diago had come to his help in the canteen at Corte, and felt sad.

At dawn they were all awake. They stretched themselves and ate some of their rations. Again they spoke little, but they were soon ready to move off. There was a low mist hanging over the plain, but it began to lift after they had marched only a short distance. Suddenly, Deval called a halt. Cato looked up to see what had caused the stoppage, and saw distant black smoke. It curled its way into the sky like a streak of black paint that had been split on to a blue canvas. It was a long way off, but it was un-mistakable. He turned and caught Sasous' eye. Neither man spoke, but their thoughts were the same. Hakim's men had got to the outpost before them!

Deval marched forward again. The men

responded. It took all morning to cover the ground to the outpost. The black smoke hung in the air tantalising them with its suggestion of a closeness that didn't exist. They had to weave their way around the scrub and bushes, and over the wadis. They sweated, cursed and toiled. As they got closer to the post, they saw the birds of prey, that advertise death, hovering in the sky. Then they saw the remains of the burned out vehicles, and smelled the stench of burning rubber and oil that was being carried to them with the hot breeze. It was an unpleasant, depressing stench, and hung heavy in their nostrils. They walked with less enthusiasm. Greco pointed to two vultures hovering over some unfortunate creature out on the plain, about a kilometre away from the post. It was not on their line of march, but close enough for them to make a detour. Deval led them, silently, towards the birds. As they drew closer to them, they saw a figure lying on the ground. They increased their pace. The figure took shape. They recognised it as the white robed figure of a man lying face downwards.

'Zugi?' Hessler asked.

They had all been thinking the same. Was it Zugi? Had Hakim's men got to him?

They came to the body and their fears were confirmed. It was Zugi! They saw his blood spattered robe, and the bloody mess where his head had been brutally clubbed from behind.

Greco kicked at the sand, angrily. 'What a bloody country,' he hissed.

'Cover him up,' Bouchier ordered. 'With anything. Move it!'

The men moved quickly. They wrapped his body in his robe and covered him with anything they could lay their hands on. Bouchier didn't give them time to dwell on his murder. As soon as he was satisfied with the burial, he marched them out. They marched towards the outpost. Cato wondered what else they would find. He saw the bearded Sergeant Villier waiting for them with a group of legionnaires. He also saw the hallmarks of a surprise attack. The vehicles were still burning and the area was strewn with debris and rubbish. There was no flagpole with the *Tri-colore*. There was no forward look-out posts; no tents. They were all burning ashes. Only the stores building and water bunker were intact.

They marched into the area and Cato saw six legionnaires lying side by side on the ground with a canvas sheet covering their faces. He could also see a dead camel in the middle of the valley, being attacked by a flock of birds, but he saw no dead natives. The legionnaires from the post stood silently watching, in various states of dress. Most of them wore steel helmets and had a sullen, dazed look on their faces, but not all of them. The white *képi* was still in evidence and one or two of them had a defiant, arrogant stance. Pedrides was one of them. He stood apart from the others with his white hat tilted to the back of his head, and a bandolier of cartridges strapped across his chest. He gripped the barrel of his rifle in an aggressive, cock-a-hoop pose. There was nothing dazed, or sullen, about him. He had the look of a man who was in full control of himself, and was enjoying the situation.

Cato saw him immediately he entered the encampment, but his thoughts at that particular moment had not been of Pedrides or of his conflict with the man. He had been thinking of Diago and Fritz, and how little hope there now seemed to be of getting help to them. He saw Pedrides, but Pedrides was for another time. Fritz and Diago were for the present.

'Spread yourselves out!' Bouchier shouted. 'Watch your fronts!'

The men started to disperse and take cover.

'Vasey! Cato!' Bouchier called. 'Get the canteens filled.'

Cato took off his pack and gave it to Sasous. Sasous handed him his canteen.

'With ice,' he pleaded.

Cato collected some of the men's canteens. Vasey did the same. They went to the sand bagged bunker which protected the water tank. In the *hole* alongside it they saw several dead natives lying on the rocks. That was the other side of the score sheet, Cato thought, grimly. Soon the stench of death would be stronger than that of the burning debris.

They entered the bunker. The air inside was still, but cooler. They started to fill the canteens.

'When will they be back?' Vasey asked.

'Soon,' Cato sighed. 'They can't afford to wait. Once they get their supplies distributed, they'll be back.'

'The valley seems deserted, yet I can kinda' feel them.'

Cato handed Vasey some of the canteens. Vasey went to distribute them. Cato continued filling the remaining canteens.

'So you came back,' a voice drawled in a slow, American accent of the southern states.

Cato froze. There was no mistaking the accent, or the identity of the man who had spoken. It was Pedrides; and there was to be no pretence this time. Cato turned and saw Pedrides watching him with a fixed, sardonic smile on his lips, and a glint in his cold, grey eyes. He was leaning, casually, against the sand bagged wall, just as he had stood in the bank. Cato felt his anger surge through his body. Instinctively, he went for his rifle.

'I wouldn't,' Pedrides snapped. He had his own rifle in his hands and the muzzle was pointing at Cato. Cato stood still and controlled his temper. He saw the glint in Pedrides' eyes and the smile on his lips. It was a look he had not seen before. It was the look of a killer – the look of a man who enjoyed killing!

'I'm glad you came back, Mister Carter,' Pedrides drawled, mockingly emphasising Cato's name.

'You remembered,' Cato hissed.

'I found out, man,' Pedrides laughed. 'The grapevine, man. It works both ways.'

'You bloody murderer,' Cato growled. 'My family!'

Pedrides gave a half laugh. Cato moved, angrily, towards him.

'I'll shoot!' Pedrides called out, hurriedly, and gesticulated with his rifle. Again Cato hesitated. 'I'll shoot,' Pedrides warned again.

'You won't get away with it, Pedrides,' Cato fumed. 'I'll see that you are brought to justice.'

Pedrides gave a laugh of derision.

'You don't dig it, man,' he scoffed.

'Dig what?' Cato hissed.

'I'm going to kill you, man.'

Cato grunted his scorn of the remark. Pedrides laughed again and then his face became serious.

'There's going to be a lot of shooting, man,' he said. 'The black power boys will be back.'

His eyes had gone cold and his lips tightly pressed, but abruptly he gave a chuckle of delight and raised his eyebrows, questioningly. 'You dig it now, man?' he asked.

Cato understood. Pedrides was threatening to kill him in the heat of the fighting. A stray bullet in the mêlée. Who would know? 'That's all you're good for,' he snarled. 'A bullet in the back. That's your pitch, but be careful the natives don't get you first.'

'Not me,' Pedrides grinned. 'I can take care of myself. This is my scene. The black boys don't frighten me. It's easy man.'

His scene! Easy! Cato's disgust made him suddenly snap. Wildly, he lashed out at Pedrides with the canteen of water that he had been holding in his hand. The canteen caught Pedrides on the side of his face, and the strap knocked the rifle out of his hand. Pedrides fell back against the sand bagged wall. Cato immediately dropped the canteen and lunged at him before he had time to recover. He pulled him away from the wall, and furiously crashed his fist into his face. Pedrides smashed against the wall again. Again, Cato pulled him away and smashed his fist into his face, and again. Pedrides went sprawling to the ground, with blood pouring out of his nostrils, but he had fallen alongside his rifle, and Cato made the mistake of not following through with his foot. In a flash, Pedrides had his rifle in his hands and was pointing it at Cato. There was no need to warn Cato that he would shoot if Cato moved. It was written on his face and in his blazing eyes. The two men stood eyeing each other, silently, both breathing heavily. Pedrides wiped the blood from his nose and slowly picked himself up. Cato watched him carefully. Pedrides backed away and picked up his white hat.

'I'll kill you if it's the last thing I do,' he blazed. 'So help me, I'll kill you.'

'Get out,' Cato snarled. 'My back isn't turned yet.'

Pedrides shook his head in uncontrolled anger, but he backed out of the bunker. Cato watched him leave. He knew that Pedrides' threat was real enough. If Pedrides wanted to save his hide, he would have to get rid of Cato, but Cato had no fear of him. Neither of Pedrides the man, nor of his threat. He felt unusually calm and at peace with himself. He was ready for anything Pedrides might attempt.

He collected the canteens. Vasey came back into the bunker. There was a puzzled expression on his face. Cato tried to forestall any questions.

'This is the last,' he said. 'Let's go.'

'What was the matter with that guy?' he

asked, with a movement of his head.

'Too much sun,' Cato said, and left the bunker before Vasey could ask any more questions. He hurried back to the men and distributed the canteens. When he came to Sasous, Sasous looked at him anxiously.

'O.K.,' Sasous asked.

'Sure,' Cato said. 'Everything is now O.K.' He gave Sasous his canteen. 'But no ice,' he added.

'*C'est la vie*,' Sasous sighed.

Cato took up a position alongside him. He didn't look to see where Pedrides was. He knew that the danger would come when the shooting started again. He saw Deval talking to Sergeant Villier, and he was concerned again for Diago and Fritz. So were the rest of the men. They watched Deval suspiciously. He was out of earshot of most of them, but not from Greco and Berge. They overheard the conversation and whispered it along the line.

'They came in the night,' the Sergeant explained. 'We saw the caravan out on the plain and kept it under surveillance. They made camp about five miles out. They attacked without warning.'

'Your casualties?' Deval asked.

'Six dead and two wounded.'

'Did you get a message through to the *poste*?'

'No, *mon Lieutenant*. They burned down

235

the radio tent first. Their attack was sudden and unexpected.'

'You should always be prepared!' Deval snapped.

'Yes, *mon Lieutenant.* We had previously reported the caravan to the *poste.*'

'When are you expected to report again?'

'My orders are to report every twenty-four hours, unless something suspicious, or unusual, occurs. I am not due to report to the *poste* again until 1800 hours this evening.'

Deval frowned. Unless the *poste* attempted to contact the outpost, they would not become suspicious until that evening, he thought, and by then it could be too late.

'What about Captain Kubik's Section?' he asked.

'He sent his scout to the outpost yesterday to inform us that he was turning south to cover the range between the outpost and the border. He had found nothing in the north.'

Deval's lips twisted into a faint smile. So Kubik had found nothing in the north, he thought. He had gone into Hakim's territory and found nothing. Hakim's men had given him the slip, but not so Deval. He had found them.

'We have no communication with anybody?' Deval asked.

'No, *mon Lieutenant.*'

The question and the answer was quickly passed around the men. They were alone,

and without means of getting help to anyone. Diago and Fritz were as good as dead!
'The caravan was carrying much needed stores for Hakim,' Deval told the Sergeant. 'He is on the move. He intends to attack the *poste*, but first he must pass this position. He needs our water.'

'We could pull out and make for the *poste*, *mon Lieutenant*,' the Sergeant suggested.

'No,' Deval replied. 'We will stop Hakim here.'

'But he has many more men, *mon Lieutenant*.'

'Half starved, poorly equipped, and badly trained.'

The Sergeant was not being put off.

'If we try to make for the *poste*, *mon Lieutenant*,' he said, 'we might come across one of our reconnaissance vehicles. They will have patrols out. Or even one of our helicopters.'

The men heard his reasoning and waited for Deval's answer. But Deval would not be sidetracked. His mind was made up.

'Hakim has camels,' he said. 'They would attack us on the plain. We have a better chance of defending ourselves here. Hakim needs access to the well. This is the only well between his base and the *poste*. We stay!'

'We could send a small patrol – say two men. They might get through, *mon Lieutenant*.'

'We are going to need every man here,' Deval retorted.

The men gritted their teeth. Deval had not given a thought to Diago and Fritz. It was only his personal quest for glory. They hated his guts.

'What rations do you have?' Deval asked.

'The fuel dump is intact. We have gasoline, ammunition, and food.'

'And weapons?'

'Two '52 machine guns and twelve automatic rifles, *mon Lieutenant*.'

'And the mortars?' Deval asked.

'They were mounted on the vehicles, *mon Lieutenant*. They were destroyed with the vehicles.'

Deval was not put off by the loss of the mortars.

'We can still last out for some time,' he said.

He didn't wait for an answer. He called Sergeant Bouchier to him.

'We can hold off any attack,' he said, with confidence. 'We brought two machine guns with us and there are two here, and we have our grenades.'

He studied the ground. Behind him was the sharp, sloping ground at the foot of the mountain. The look-out post was on a ledge where the slope met the vertical face of the mountain. Above that the mountain side rose high into the sky. They would not attack from there, he thought. He saw the sand-bagged water point and the ammunition dump tucked neatly into the mountain side. They were also safe, he thought. Hakim's men would have to cross the *hole* to get to them. He looked at the spur that hid the head of the valley from his view and gave their position its harbour-like shape. That would be the danger point, he thought. That and the dried up river bed that meandered its way through the valley about a hundred metres in front of their position.

'Send somebody to the look-out post,' he ordered. 'The rest of the men are to dig in and prepare two lines of defence.'

He gave his orders decisively, indicating the positions of each position and the arc of fire of the machine guns. They formed two lines of fire. On the forward slopes, he placed two machine gun positions, one on either flank. Sergeant Villier and half his Section were to be on the left flank with one of their machine guns. They had the spur as their target and were covering the *hole*. On the other flank Hessler and Berge were to set up their machine gun to cover an attack from the plain.

The second line of defence was to be higher up the slope, spread evenly along the front. On the right flank Sergeant Bouchier and Greco were to site their machine gun. On the left flank the other men of Sergeant

Villier's Section were to set up their machine gun. The rest of the men were to be spread along the line on the higher ground with four metres between each position.

'They will probably attack at night,' Deval said. He turned to Sergeant Villier. 'Set up some warning system. Use tin cans – anything that will make a noise.'

'Yes, *mon Lieutenant.*'

Deval dismissed the two Sergeants. The Sergeants gave out their orders. Irish was sent to the look-out. The rest of the men started preparing their defences. Cato worked alongside Sasous and Vasey. They scratched, angrily, at the surface with shovels and hand tools under the blazing sun.

Bouchier came to inspect their position.

'What about Diago and Fritz?' Sasous asked.

'What about them?' Bouchier growled. 'Do you want to go back for them?'

'We could send somebody to the *poste,*' Cato suggested.

'Do you think Hakim's men aren't watching?' Bouchier snapped. 'How far do you think anyone would get?'

He glowered at them all, but the men had lost their fear of him.

'We could all make for the *poste,*' Sasous said, still scratching at his hole. 'It would only be one day's hard march.'

'And let Hakim get through?'

'He'll get through in any case,' Sasous replied.

'Over our dead bodies,' Hook growled.

'Then get plenty of rocks for cover, Hook,' Bouchier said. 'Unless you want the vultures picking at your bones.'

Hook turned his back on the Sergeant and worked, angrily, on his position. So did Cato and the others. Fritz and Diago had been written off just like Napoleon, Schnell, and Zugi, had been. Cato silently cursed Deval and his lust for glory.

The men finished preparing their positions and waited patiently for Hakim to appear. Their cursed the heat and wondered what to expect, but they took heart in their defences and their fire power.

Deval also waited patiently. He crouched in his pit close to Berge and Hessler and studied the distant slopes with his binoculars. He covered the yellow, brown rocks and the dirty green shrubs carefully. He knew Hakim's men were there. He could feel them. Perhaps they were also waiting for the dark, he thought. Well, he had prepared for that also. He let the binoculars hang around his neck and he leaned against the edge of his pit. He felt the same tingle of excitement pass through his body, that he had felt earlier, and he enjoyed the feeling. It stimulated him and made the blood rush through his veins.

Cato sat looking across the valley. It reminded him of a vacation that he had once spent touring Arizona. There was the same desert scrub, and heat, that he had encountered there, and the same feeling about the terrain that it would absorb all life and yield nothing. But in the States he had been in a motor car on a highway and he had driven hurriedly away from its harsh struggle for survival. Now he was part of it and there was no running away. He picked up a handful of small, loose stones and thoughtfully threw them away one by one. He missed the States, he thought. He missed it very much. He missed his work and the way of life that he had been used to. He would like to get back to it again. He could cope now. He would like to get out of the Legion and he would like to see Jaquie again. She had often been in his thoughts as he had silently marched. With Jaquie, he knew that he could start again. As he thought about her, his eyes looked along the line to where Pedrides was dug in. He was with two other legionnaires from Sergeant Villier's Section at the end of their line, overlooking the *hole* and stores dump. He was sitting in his trench with his back to the wall, cleaning his rifle. Cato frowned and looked away. His feelings for Pedrides had become strangely numbed. He didn't feel the great hatred, or need for revenge any longer. He had finally got rid of them when he had crashed his fist into Pedrides' face, but it hadn't been that one act alone that had drained him of his feelings, he thought. It had been a combination of many things. It had been Jaquie and her gentleness. It had been the constant burning sun that made everything a battle. It had been the physical strain of the previous day's march, the sight of Napoleon's dead body – and Schnell's and Zugi's, and the thought of Diago and Fritz being left alone on the plain. They had all helped. They had all pressed down on him like a heavy weight on a spring and like a spring losing its recoil he had lost his need for revenge. His confrontation with Pedrides had just been the final act to get it out of his system. It had satisfied a basic need in him to inflict some physical pain on Pedrides.

The other men also had their own personal thoughts as they sat behind their pile of rocks under the blazing heat of the sun. There was no conversation and no movement. A silence settled over the area, until it was rudely broken by Irish.

'Hakim!' he shouted from his look-out position. 'Hakim!'

Deval had also seen some movement. He studied it through his binoculars. The rest of the men turned to stare at the mountains across the valley. They began to see waves of movement – sudden movement of small groups of indistinguishable figures, and then a pause followed by more movement. The whole mountain side seemed to be on the move.

'*Mon Dieu!*' Greco exclaimed. '*Regardez! –* there are hundreds of them!'

A tremor passed through Cato's body and the adrenalin surged through his blood stream. The whole mountain side seemed to be on the move. They were facing an army!

Hessler gripped his machine gun, nervously, and looked through his sights. Berge felt his innards turn over.

'Don't waste your ammunition,' Bouchier called out. 'They are well out of range.'

The men rested their automatics and stared across the broad valley plain. They saw the wave of figures reach the foot of the mountains and disappear amongst the scrub and bushes. They seemed to be swallowed up by the ground.

Sergeant Bouchier studied them through a pair of binoculars and knew, instantly, that they were not facing a band of savages. Nor were they facing an untrained, marauding band of terrorists. They were facing a disciplined army! Hakim's men were even wearing a form of khaki uniform! Again Deval had miscalculated. Again Deval had misled them. Bouchier felt an anger towards Deval that he had never felt before towards an officer of the Legion. Deval had bungled the whole operation.

Crump! Crump! Two clouds of earth rose into the sky as two explosions burst the banks of the wadi in front of their position.

'*Mon Dieu!*' Bouchier hissed. 'Mortars!'

Mortars! The word came to the men like an electric shock. Hakim's men had mortars! Mortars! My God! Bouchier thought again. They were all like sitting ducks waiting to be picked off.

Crump! Crump! Crump! Three more explosions rent the air.

The men felt an ice-cold chill pass through their bodies as they watched the river bed explode and throw up its bed of dirty, yellow sand. They quickly put on their steel helmets.

Two more quick bursts shattered the far bank of the river wadi. They were falling short of their target, about a hundred and fifty metres short. Was that the limit of their range? Bouchier wondered.

He grabbed his binoculars and scoured the range of mountains. He saw further waves of Hakim's men move down the slope, but no mortar positions.

Brrr!... Brrr!... Brr!

Hessler let loose a stream of bullets. Bouchier watched their tracers scream across the plain. They tailed away in the distance short of the advancing troops. They were still out of range. Deval shouted to Hessler to cease firing. He turned and waved Bouchier to him. He also called Sergeant Villier. Bouchier slid down the hillside. Sergeant Villier crept along the line.

'They aren't firing their mortars from the far side,' Deval said. 'That means they are coming from our left flank. From the head of the valley. They are using the spur for cover.'

Bouchier grunted his agreement. They were firing from beyond the spur.

'Fortunately, they can't get our positions from there,' Deval said.

'If they move out, we can get them with our machine guns,' Sergeant Villier said, 'and if they move to the far bank of the valley we will be out of their range.'

'They will probably make for the river bed,' Deval said, 'but first they will have to get their infantry close enough to give them cover. If we can cut down their infantry, we can stop them. As soon as their infantry are in range, we must stop them. If they get those mortars close enough...' He didn't have to explain the consequences. The two Sergeants had seen action before. They returned to their positions and briefed their men.

'As soon as they are in range, fire,' Bouchier ordered. 'You must stop them bringing their mortars into position.'

'Let's hope they have no bloody artillery

as well,' Greco shouted out.

'You would have heard them by now,' Bouchier shouted back.

Brrrrr!... Brrr!... Brrrr!

Sergeant Villier's two machine guns joined in. A stream of tracers and a trail of lead fanned its way across the valley. The movement in the valley stopped.

Cato and the others lay behind their rifles and watched their front. They saw a small group of figures running, at a crouch, to their right flank.

'Brr!... Brrrrr!... Brr!... Brrrr!

A hail of lead followed them. One figure fell. The rest disappeared into the ground.

Cato and the others watched, tensely, every nerve strained, looking for a moving figure. They were now fighting for survival. The uniformed figures that they had seen as blurred specks in the distance, were now becoming distinguishable.

The mortars opened up again.

Crump! Crump! Crump! Crump!

A rain of bombs landed on the near side of the river bed blowing up a cloud of dust.

Brrr!... Brrr!... Brrrrr!... Brr!... Brrrr!

Hessler fired through the cloud screen.

Sergeant Villier's machine guns did the same.

Brrr!... Brrrr!... Brr!

Suddenly a stream of bullets smacked into the side of the mountain below Bouchier's section. Cato and the others instantly took cover. The enemy had got one of their own machine guns into position.

Brrr!... Brrrr! Brr!... Brrrr! Brr!

Bouchier opened up. But more bullets came smacking into their position from the enemy's guns. Hessler joined the duel. He had seen the firing position. Cato and the others kept their heads down. Bullets were ricocheting off the rocks and whining over their heads.

Sergeant Villier's guns blasted across the valley, towards the spur.

Crump! Crump! Crump!

Again a row of mortar bombs dropped short, but raised a cloud of sand. Hessler and Bouchier kept firing at the enemy's machine gun. The men followed suit, one by one. Bouchier's gun went silent. So did Hessler's. There was no response from the enemy machine gun position. Hessler and Bouchier had done their job. A sudden hail of bullets sprayed into their positions from the spur. Furiously Bouchier shouted loudly to Sergeant Villier.

'On the spur!'

Sergeant Villier saw the firing position and his machine gun retaliated, but one of his men had been hit.

Crump! Crump! Crump! Crump!

A further barrage of bombs fell on the plain. Another cloud of dust formed a screen.

Again Hessler and Bouchier fired into the dust. Sergeant Villier's guns had made the enemy on the spur withdraw, but they kept up a sniping action.

Cato fired wildly into the dust screen and at the spur. Bullets smacked into the ground above his head and made him crouch behind his rocks. Vasey gave a sudden cry. Cato turned and saw him lying on his side.

Crump! Crump! Crump!

'Keep firing!' Bouchier yelled. 'Keep firing!'

Cato saw Vasey move and pick up his rifle. Cato turned to his front and fired blindly into the dust screen again. Their machine guns were also blasting away, but bullets were also whining into their positions and ricocheting off the rocks. Cato kept his head low and fired between his rocks, but he could see little of the enemy for the dusty haze. He emptied his magazine and refilled it as if desperate to be rid of his ammunition.

'*Cessez le feu!*' Bouchier suddenly shouted. 'Cease firing!'

The men didn't all hear him. He moved along the line.

'*Cessez le feu!*' he yelled again. 'Stop!'

The firing died away.

Cato put down his rifle and felt his body sag. The immediate crisis was over. He wanted to laugh and cry. To shout – to get up and run about. He wanted to get away from his pile of rocks. He was still alive. Thank God! he thought. Thank God!

Suddenly he remembered that Vasey had been hit! What about Sasous? He turned, anxiously, to look at Sasous. Sasous was still alive! He was lying with his back to the wall. He was looking at Cato. He gave a smile and a flick of his hand. Cato waved back, and hurriedly crawled to Vasey's position. Vasey was lying on his side. There was bleeding from his shoulder. He gave an apologetic smile.

'How is it?' Cato asked.

'Somebody winged me,' Vasey replied. 'Just a flesh wound.'

'You'll be O.K.'

'Sure.'

Bouchier came along the line and saw the situation.

'I'll put on a field dressing,' Cato said.

'Fix him good,' Bouchier growled. 'We need every man. Those bastards will be back.'

'It was from the spur,' Vasey grumbled.

Cato ripped open Vasey's shirt and exposed the wound. The bullet had gone straight through his shoulder. He got a field bandage and powdered and dressed the wound. But it was only a stop gap arrangement. Vasey would soon need proper medical attention.

'Thanks, Cato,' Vasey said.

Cato patted him on the helmet and turned away. He found himself looking directly towards Pedrides' position. Pedrides was still alive, but one of the legionnaires beside was dead. The other was crouched behind his machine gun. Pedrides turned his head and his eyes met and held Cato's. Pedrides held up his rifle, pointedly, and smiled. Cato looked away and crawled back to his own position.

'How is Vasey?' Sasous called out. He was lying with his back to his pile of rocks smoking a cigarette. He had exchanged his steel helmet for his bush hat and it hid part of his face.

'He'll live,' Cato replied, 'but Bouchier won't be bothering him for some time.'

'That's some compensation at least.'

'How about you? You O.K.?'

Sasous lifted his hat from his eyes and looked at Cato.

'I could think of a lot of other places I'd rather be,' he smiled, 'including the bedchamber of that Madame in Bonifacio.' He put his hat over his face again. 'This heat,' he sighed.

'Yeah!' Cato agreed. 'It's bloody hot.'

He looked up at the sun. It was like a ball of fire, but it would soon be starting its descent. The worst would soon be over for the day. Was that the same with Hakim's men? he wondered. Was their worst over? Or was there still more to come? He waited to find out.

Hakim's men also seemed to be waiting. The heat of the day was unbearable. The horizon shimmered and wavered as the earth baked. Only the birds of prey hovered in the clear blue sky, but they kept their distance from both camps.

It was a long, tortuous afternoon, but for Deval it was a breathing space and a time to plan. He knew that he had to do something to protect their position. Hakim's men could move up in the dark and overrun them. He studied the ground and knew that the river bed would be their target. Once they were massed in there, they could launch an all out attack. They had to be stopped somehow. He glanced along his line and saw their dead legionnaires under a canvas cover beside the dump. The dump! If Hakim's men got into the dump it would go up like a bomb, he thought grimly. The gasoline would... He abruptly stopped thinking about the dump and thought about the gasoline... Suddenly he had an idea. He turned and waved Sergeant Bouchier and Sergeant Villier to him. The two sergeants scrambled into his position.

'Hakim's men will move forward when it is dark,' he said. 'They will probably take up their positions in the river bed. There is plenty of cover for them.'

'We can move our own troops into the river bed,' Bouchier said.

'No,' Deval replied. 'I have a better idea. Which direction is the breeze?'

'From the mountains to the plain, *mon Lieutenant.*'

Deval nodded his head in agreement. 'So if we set fire to the valley it would not carry back towards our position.'

The two Sergeants grunted their agreement.

'If we pour our gasoline over the ground on the far bank of the river and light it...' He left the rest unsaid. 'We could have two men forward ready to set it off,' he added. 'It would go up like a balloon.'

He turned his back, momentarily, on the Sergeants. He got great personal satisfaction out of his superiority over his N.C.O.'s and it reflected in his face He didn't want them to see it. He knew the picture was slowly going through their brains. They were thinking of any obstacles. Deval had already done that. He turned to face them again.

'First we prepare a second line of defence, in case the mortars get our positions in their range,' he explained. 'We move one machine gun forward beyond the river bed. That will keep them quiet. As soon as it gets dark we send out patrols with the gasoline. We saturate the ground on the far bank of the river and in the river bed itself. We will have an ignition point on our left flank, forward of our position. We will pull the machine gun back and let Hakim's men move forward. Then we will ignite the gasoline, but we don't want the area ignited too soon. We must wait until they are in position. We can put out some trips to warn us. There must be no premature firing into the area, or it will go up.'

He looked at the two Sergeants.

'Any questions?'

'They will smell it, *mon Lieutenant*,' Bouchier warned.

'Not so long as there is rubber burning,' Deval replied. 'Nothing can be stronger than that stench. See that it continues to burn.'

'Yes, *mon Lieutenant*.'

'Anything else?'

'No, *mon Lieutenant*,' they replied.

'Good.'

The two N.C.O.'s retreated. Sergeant Villier was to go forward and keep the enemy pinned to the foot of the mountains across the plain. Bouchier would organise the gasoline.

Bouchier briefed his men, but they couldn't move forward until dark. They saw Sergeant Villier and two of his legionnaires creep forward, as they set about improving their defences. They gathered rocks and sandbags from the demolished forward look-out post and built a protective wall around themselves. They also prepared a second line of defence on the higher ground and they buried their dead. It was slow work and the men were careful not to expose themselves as a target for a sniper for any long periods. Pedrides also worked with Bouchier's men, but he kept his distance from Cato. When they finished, they returned to their original positions and watched the sun slowly drop to the horizon, glad of the peace, but hesitant of the cool of the evening and the activity that would follow.

No sooner had dusk arrived than Bouchier took over again. Before the blanket of darkness fully descended, he had the men detailed to a specific activity and certain area of ground, but he waited until the darkness fell before ordering them to move.

When they moved, they moved swiftly. They collected their cans of gasoline from the dump and crept forward to the river bed. Sergeant Villier opened up with his machine gun on the far bank of the river bed and sprayed the ground ahead of him at irregular intervals. The men quickly spread their inflammable liquid over the dried bushes, the scrub, and the coarse grass.

Greco and Hook had been detailed to the forward ignition point and they quickly dug a position on the left flank, close to the river bed. They were to be joined by Sergeant

Villier when his men were pulled back. Their signal to light the gasoline was a green flare, or a verbal order from Lieutenant Deval or Sergeant Bouchier. They were then to return to their positions in the line.

Cato and the others returned their empty cans to the dump and returned to their positions. Irish had left the look-out position and was dug in alongside Vasey. The sky was clear, the moon was still Islamic shaped, but there was a hint of yellow in the darkness that gave an eerie atmosphere. Sergeant Villier gave a final burst and crept back through the burning area and took up his position with Greco and Hook. His other two legionnaires fell back to their new position in the line. The men prepared themselves for the cold of the night, and waited.

Time passed slowly. No one spoke. Occasionally Bouchier made a tour of the line, but never spoke to anyone. He just reassured himself that all was well. At midnight there was still no movement, but gradually the feeling that Hakim's men were on the move began to creep over the men. Their nerves began to tingle, as if pricked by a sixth sense. They braced themselves and looked at each other in the darkness. Cato glanced at Vasey who gave a wave of his hand. He had suffered during the heat of the afternoon, but he had picked up with the cool of the evening. He lay sideways again, his wall supporting his wounded shoulder. Sasous also moved his head, as if to indicate that he sensed the movement of Hakim's men. They looked to their front, but saw only the dark shapes of the bushes. Nervously they fingered their triggers.

A faint distant tinkle of a can gave a tell-tale sign. It carried across the still night. The men heard it again. Their mouths dried up. Even the toughest of them felt the anticipation. Deval also felt it. His body shivered, but his eyes were wide and his face flushed. The feeling gripped him like nothing he had felt before. He welcomed it. It was his narcotic.

More sounds came from the crude warning system. More tinkling from the cans. Deval ordered Hessler to fire high to miss the burning area. If they didn't open fire, Hakim's men would become suspicious. Hessler opened up. The rest held back and watched his tracer bullets streak across the sky line, curling away in the distance. He ceased firing. There was no reply from across the valley. They listened. Suddenly a trip flare was set off giving a red glow, but there was no obvious sign of movement. Hakim's men were keeping to the ground. Hessler fired again. He kept firing short bursts. So did the other machine guns. The rest of the men waited nervously.

Crump! A mortar exploded on the rocks below the section. Instantly the men flung themselves to the ground as a shower of rocks spattered the area. Crump! Crump! Crump! Three more explosives landed in the area. The men hugged the ground. There was a yell and a cry. Hessler opened up again. He fired a burst across the ground. So did the other machine guns. Bullets were streaking across the sky. But they were coming both ways. Some smacked into their positions. They were coming from the spur. The machine gun in Pedrides' position retaliated.

Crump! Crump! Crump! Crump!

The ground started exploding all around the men. Cato hugged the earth. They would all be killed, he thought. The mortars had got their range! They had to do something quick. A rain of stones fell on top of him. Hessler wasn't firing any longer.

'I can't see!' someone yelled. It sounded like Berge. 'I can't see!' the voice yelled again.

Suddenly a green flash pierced the darkness. It was the signal to ignite the gasoline. Almost instantly there was a flash and a strip of orange burst on the horizon.

Crump! Crump! Crump!

Three more mortars landed on the rocks below where Cato was lying. The shattered rocks rained over the section. There was another flash and the sky became an orange glow, as a sheet of flame burst along the river bed. The whole plain seemed to be aflame. The sky was all orange. It lit up the whole area. The men peered over their walls. They could see the river bed and the far bank. They were both a flaming inferno. Then came the cries. Piercing, agonising cries of pain. Not one or two, but several. The men saw figures start running back across the valley, some with the flames coming from their bodies. There were too many to count. It was a mass retreat.

'Fire at them!' Bouchier shouted. 'Fire at them! Fire!'

One by one the men opened up. They fired at the figures and saw some of them fall. Bouchier's machine gun tore into the flames adding a hail of death to the furnace. Cato looked at the burning plain and saw the running figures being torn down by the bullets, and looked away. He saw that Sasous had also turned away, but the orange glow stayed and the firing continued. The machine guns sprayed the plain and took their toll. After about five minutes continuous firing, they abruptly ceased. The orange glow remained, but there were no cries of pain. The legionnaires lay beside their guns and watched the flickering flames. They saw two men come out of the hole that had been the ignition position. A third was being carried. The party made their way back to the line and took up a position on the right flank.

Bouchier scrambled along the line. In the

dull glow his features looked grotesque. His face and beard were spotted with dirt from the mortar explosions.

'They'll still be coming,' he warned, quickly, and moved on. 'Keep alert and get your grenades ready.'

'Any casualties?' someone shouted.

'Yes,' Vasey shouted out. 'Irish got it.'

Irish dead! Their numbers were slowly being reduced, Cato thought, as he un-clipped his grenades from his webbing. Another barrage from the mortars and they would all be dead. A feeling of despair passed through his body. It all seemed so unnecessary. The screams from the burning natives had unnerved him. He could still hear their cries of agony and a faint whimper still occasionally carried across the plain. And the smell of smoke irritated his nostrils. He lay forward against his own wall, his eyes blurred from the lack of sleep, and he watched the smouldering plain. He could see the river bed and follow its meandering course. On the far bank were small pockets of fires where some of the bushes were still burning. Beyond that was a dark blanket where the orange glow faded into the dark sky. He looked below him to where Hessler, Berge and Deval were sited. He saw Bouchier with Deval. He saw them move to Hessler's position and pull some-one out. It could have been Hessler or

Berge. He didn't know who. He saw three figures move up the slope, but he lost them as they climbed into a position along the line. He glanced to his left flank and saw Pedrides and the other legionnaire.

'Ammunition?'

It was Greco. He was at Vasey's position. He threw some pouches to him and moved to Cato.

'Who got it?' Cato asked.

'Hessler, Irish and some of the other men,' Greco said. 'It was their mortars that did it. Sergeant Villier is also wounded. He's with Bouchier.'

Hessler, Cato thought. The Legion had lost a good soldier. 'What about Berge?' he asked.

'He's got a head wound, but he'll be all right.'

Greco threw some pouches to him.

'We'll soon all be dead at this rate,' he growled.

'Perhaps they won't attack again,' Cato suggested.

'Not according to Deval. He thinks they are like a dying animal. Their last fling.'

'He's a *cochon*,' Sasous said. 'He'll be enjoying this.'

Greco threw some pouches to him as he moved along the line.

'Poor Irish,' Vasey said.

Cato saw him shuffle, uncomfortably, in

261

his hole.

Crack! A bullet whined into their positions. They kept their heads down.

'Somebody is still about,' Sasous grumbled.

There was a burst from Pedrides' machine gun. They were firing at the spur. The tracers screamed into the rocks and then there was silence again.

'Poor Irish,' Vasey said again. 'I'm going to miss him.'

'Yeah,' Cato agreed, 'and Hessler.'

Vasey started emptying the cartridges from his pouches.

'There is an address inside my helmet, Cato,' he said, without looking at Cato. 'If anything happens...' He left the rest unsaid and continued to empty his pouches with his head downcast. 'How about you?' he asked. 'Anybody?'

Anybody? Cato turned away. He had no family now, he thought. There were a few relations, but he hadn't kept in touch. There was nobody who would really care, except Jaquie. Jaquie would care, he thought. She would be sad. If he lived he would go to her. If he didn't there was nobody else who would care.

'There might be,' he sighed. 'If we ever get out of this.'

'You'll see her again,' Sasous said. 'I know.'

Cato didn't say anything, but Sasous' remark gave him encouragement. There was something about Sasous that Cato felt he could trust. Sasous had that effect on him.

'Remember *The Gypsy,*' Sasous said.

'*The Gypsy?*' Cato mused. He had forgotten about him. *The Gypsy* had said that he was going to *travel*. 'Some travelling,' he grunted. 'How about you, Sasous?' he asked.

Sasous shifted his body into a more comfortable position.

'Well, now that you mention it,' he said in an off hand manner. 'I have been thinking about my affairs during the past few hours, and I have decided that *La Légion* is not really for me.'

'So you are going to *travel?*' Cato smiled.

'Yes,' Sasous agreed. 'When this little business is over, I am going to *travel*. With my connections, *mon ami,* we can, perhaps travel together in style and go places.'

'Even to Paris?' Cato asked.

'But *certainement* – especially to Paris. Who knows? There might have been a change of *Government*. Besides it could be no more dangerous than this.'

'True enough.'

So Sasous had also come to terms with himself, Cato thought, and was glad.

'Sure Sasous,' he said. 'We'll do just that.'

Whether or not it would happen was another matter, but it gave them hope.

They settled down to their vigil and the cold of the night that gripped their bodies and made them shiver. The fires were burning low, but the stench of the burning vegetation and rubber hung heavy over the area. Many of the men smoked cigarettes. Few of them spoke. They all waited. Their eyes became heavy, their bodies tired.

As dawn approached, a damp mist started to slowly cover the plain. Cato saw it as a grey blanket as it engulfed the burning embers of the fires. He watched it roll over the river wadi towards the foot of the mountain slope and up to their positions. Then they were all engulfed in a cold dampness that made them long for the heat. Bouchier crept along the line warning them to keep awake.

'They'll use the cover,' he warned.

Cato looked over his wall. He could only see about ten metres into the grey, swirling mist and he couldn't see Pedrides! Pedrides was hidden in the mist! It made him pull himself together. He became fully alert. He ate some of his rations. He saw Sasous and Vasey doing the same.

Crump! The ground around Cato violently shook as a mortar bomb exploded beneath him, sending a shower of rocks into his position. He flung himself to the ground.

Crump! Crump! Crump!

Bombs were falling all over the area. The hill side was like an exploding mass of rocks. They had to get out of it, Cato thought desperately. They had to move! Why didn't they get the order to retreat? Suddenly Bouchier was beside him, his large frame almost on top of him. Another bomb exploded. The ground shook.

'Take this machine gun and come with me,' Bouchier shouted. He thrust the gun in Cato's hand and slung Cato's rifle over his own shoulder. He crawled out of the pit. Cato followed. They hugged the ground as two more bombs exploded behind them. Bouchier scrambled quickly down the side of the slope. Cato followed.

Crump! Crump! Crump! The bombs were hitting the area all around them. Bouchier scrambled into one of their forward positions. Cato joined him. Bouchier pulled him close.

'They have moved out from the spur,' he said. 'Keep away from the *hole*. When I start to throw these.' He held up his hand grenades. 'You fire like hell!'

He didn't wait for an answer. He moved out. Cato followed. The mist swirled about them. Behind them the mountain side was exploding with the bombs. In front of them was only the mist. They scrambled quickly along the side of the *hole,* their feet hitting the loose rocks. They came upon clear pockets without the mist and then they would be engulfed again with damp, swirling cloud. Cato kept up with Bouchier.

The perspiration rolled off his face. Bouchier hesitated. Cato came up beside him. They stood and listened. They could just hear faint muffled voices, followed by a plopping sound. Bouchier held up two grenades and pulled out the pins with his teeth. He crouched down on his belly. Cato followed suit. They crawled across the scrub. Pieces of rock dug into Cato's body, but he didn't feel them. They wormed their way between the bushes, slithering over the ground. Bouchier seemed to have his own direction finder. Suddenly, he stopped and turned to Cato.

'Right!' he hissed.

He stood up. So did Cato. Cato squeezed the trigger. The machine gun burst into life. He didn't know what he was firing at, but he sprayed the mist in front of him in a half circle. He didn't hear any cries or see Bouchier throw his grenades. All he concentrated on was firing the machine gun.

A wall of intense heat suddenly hit him and knocked him off his feet. As he was falling an explosion almost burst his ear drums. He rolled himself into a ball and covered his head. A pungent smell filled his nostrils and a hail of sand and rubble peppered his body. He moved himself and looked into a white veil. It had suddenly become dawn. It was as if the grenades had blown away the darkness that had been with the mist and left only the whiteness.

He saw Bouchier alongside him and saw that he was still wearing his gloves. He felt like laughing.

'Eeee!... Eeeee!... Eeeeeeeee!'

The piercing cry instantly chilled his innards. It had come from their lines.

Crack! Crack! Crack! A fusillade of rifle shots rang out. It was followed by another and another.

Brrr!... Brrrr!... Brr! A machine gun opened up.

All hell had been let loose. The whole plain seemed alive. There was the loud explosion of grenades and machine guns and rifles were blasting away.

'They're attacking,' Bouchier snapped, and got to his feet. Cato did the same. They ran back to the lines, through the patches of mist. Cato stumbled over a bush that tore at his legs, but he ran on. He saw half crouched, dark figures in front of him. He stopped and fired a burst from the hip. The figures fell to the ground. He carried on firing. Bouchier came alongside him and pulled at him.

'Come on!' he yelled.

Cato stopped firing. More figures appeared out of the mist. Bouchier fired at one. Cato gave a burst. The figure fell to the ground. Bouchier jumped into a hole. Cato followed him. Bouchier grabbed the machine gun from Cato and sprayed the line at the foot of the hill behind their position. There was a clear patch reaching up to their lines where a group of natives were firing at the section. As Bouchier fired, the natives turned and ran across their flanks into a patch of mist. Bouchier's gun ran out of ammunition. Furiously, Cato tore into a box that was lying at his feet. He handed a magazine to Bouchier. Bouchier loaded the gun. Cato picked up his rifle. A bullet tore into the ground alongside him. Bouchier swung around and sprayed the area. Two figures fell at the edge of their hole. He turned away and sprayed the ground at the foot of the slope, but the firing had become spasmodic. The heat had suddenly gone out of the battle. Bouchier stopped firing his machine gun. Cato lowered his sights. He felt weak. His whole body seemed to suddenly lose all its vitality. He sat down, but found himself sitting on the dead body of a native warrior. He moved away, quickly, and pulled the body out of the hole.

'You stay here,' Bouchier shouted. 'I'll go and investigate.'

He got out of the hole. Cato watched him disappear into the mist. Suddenly a bullet whined off the side of Cato's helmet! He flung himself to the ground. Crack! Another bullet smacked into the wall beside him. He felt a sudden burning sensation in his arm. He had been hit! He moved instantly.

Another bullet smacked into the hole. They were coming from up the slope! In a flash, he realised who was shooting at him. It was Pedrides! He quickly turned and saw Pedrides coming down the slope towards him. Pedrides was out to kill him! The thought electrified him. He saw Pedrides lift his arm as if to throw something. His brain told him that it was a grenade! Frantically, he lunged his body out of the ground. Wildly, he scrambled away from the area. Suddenly the ground gave way beneath him and he felt himself sliding down the *hole*. He crashed, heavily, against a boulder as the grenade exploded above him. A rain of sand fell in the *hole,* as he hurriedly picked himself up. He went for his rifle. It wasn't beside him! Desperately, he looked for it. He saw it wedged between some rocks up the side of the crater. Crack! A bullet smacked against the boulder beside him. A fragment of rock spurted into his face. He scurried behind a rock and looked up. Pedrides was standing at the top of the hole taking careful aim. He felt the blood drain from his body. Suddenly, another shot rang out, and he saw Pedrides twist his body. He had been hit! He turned and fired at someone else. Furiously, Cato scrambled up the side of the slope and grabbed his rifle. Without looking to see where he was shooting, he turned and fired and kept on firing. He looked for Pedrides as he was firing. His gun went dead. At the same instant, he saw Pedrides throw up his arms and stumble forward. He watched in a semi-daze as Pedrides fell into the *hole* and crash on to the rocks beneath him. Like a desperate animal, he went after him, but Pedrides didn't move. He lay still, face downwards. Cato turned him over with the barrel of his rifle. Pedrides' cold, grey eyes were open, but they were glazed and lifeless. Pedrides was dead!

A sudden exchange of rifle shots made Cato move. He climbed out of the hole and saw Vasey lying on the ground a short distance away from him. It had been Vasey who had fired at Pedrides, he thought. It had been Vasey who had given him his opportunity.

He darted over to him. Vasey had a pained look on his face. Pedrides had shot him in the knee. It was bleeding badly. Hurriedly, Cato put his arm around him and dragged him to the cover of some nearby rocks. He looked around him, but there was no one firing at them. The mist was clearing. He could see along the line. The shooting was only spasmodic. For the time being it was over, he thought. He turned his attention to Vasey. He was bleeding badly. Cato made a makeshift tourniquet with his dagger on Vasey's leg.

'Thanks,' he said, as he tightened the binding.

'You got him?' Vasey grimaced.

'Yes,' Cato sighed. 'I got him.'

Bouchier came darting towards them. He looked at Vasey and handed Cato a dressing. He left them and went on his rounds. Cato started to dress the wound.

'You heard him in the bunker?' he asked.

'Yeah,' Vasey grunted. 'I heard him and I saw him go for you.'

Cato finished the dressing. Vasey held his arm.

Cato looked at him. Vasey dropped his eyes.

'What is it?' Cato asked. Suddenly he expected the worse.

'It's Sasous,' Vasey muttered.

'Sasous!' Cato exclaimed, with alarm.

'He's dead, Cato.'

Dead! The blood drained out of Cato's body. Sasous dead. 'Oh! No!' he groaned. 'Not Sasous.'

He stood up to go and see that it wasn't so.

'Cato!' Vasey called, and grabbed him. 'It was a direct hit,' he said. 'A mortar bomb.'

Cato froze. He suddenly felt weak – very weak. He sat down on the ground again. Sasous was dead.

'I'm sorry,' Vasey said.

Bouchier joined them.

'It is over for the time being,' he said.

Cato stared at a dark, scarred face lying

close by. It had a splash of red at the temple where a bullet had embedded itself in the skull. It was no longer a living individual with a soul, a will, and a mind, he thought. It was dead! And so was Sasous!

'My God!' he asked. 'Why? Why?'

He stood up and looked at the bodies that lay strewn around the area. They were native bodies – black and brown – in dark brown cloaks, and ill-fitting, khaki uniforms.

'Why?' he asked again. 'Why?'

'Never mind why,' Bouchier snapped. 'Get some ammunition and get Vasey on to the higher ground. They will be back.' He threw a box of ammunition at him.

Cato shook his head. It had all been a senseless, unnecessary slaughter.

'Move it!' Bouchier snarled. 'Pronto!'

Cato looked at him. Bouchier was standing facing him.

'Get some ammunition,' Bouchier ordered.

'Damn you! Don't you have any feelings?'

'Not now,' Bouchier shouted. 'Move it! Now!'

Cato gave him a look of disgust, but took some of the bandoliers of ammunition and slung them over his shoulder.

The mist still hung over the plain, but there was more daylight. Cato could see along the section line. There were rocks and stones all over the slope. He saw the position where

Sergeant Villier's men had retreated to, and he could see Sergeant Villier – bloody and dirty – behind his wall. But he couldn't see where Sasous had been! He handed some ammunition to Vasey and saw the pain in Vasey's eyes as he moved his body. His shoulder wound had stopped bleeding, but it was paining him. Cato got him on to one foot and half carried him up the slope, and into a position close to where Pedrides had been. The other legionnaire who had been with Pedrides was still in his hole. His uniform was marked with red blood marks as if he had been peppered with shrapnel, and his eyes looked glazed, but he sat behind his gun with a fixed expression on his face.

Cato left Vasey and crawled along the line to where Sasous' hole had been. It was rocks and rubble. He saw fragments of clothing and bloody flesh. That was all that was left of Sasous. That was all that was left of his friend. He sat on the rocks and felt a great ache in the pit of his guts. Sasous had been everything to him – friend, brother, and father figure. It had been Sasous who had made the contacts for him and helped him in his search for Pedrides. It had been Sasous who had kept him going with his wit and wisdom. It had been Sasous who had made the Legion bearable for him. Without Sasous it could have been a hell. Now Sasous was dead, and he felt a great sadness well up inside him. He stood up and went back to Vasey.

'He will be happy now,' Vasey said.

Cato took a breath. 'Yeah,' he said. 'He'll be in his Paris now.'

'Cato!'

It was Bouchier calling. He was with Deval. Cato automatically reacted and stood up. He was a disciplined legionnaire. He saw the mist rolling away leaving a score of dead native bodies strewn over the ground. He looked at their own positions. He saw that Hook was also dead – his body lay lifeless on a heap of rocks. He gritted his teeth. Hook had been coarse and tough, but he had been one of them, and he hadn't wanted to die on a pile of rocks in a senseless battle. Neither had Sasous. None of them had, but they weren't the only dead. There were only three of Sergeant Villier's former Section still alive and one of them was badly wounded. And their Sergeant was also wounded. Their comrades lay dead in their positions. So did Hessler. He lay on his back with his face to the sun, but his eyes had been closed. He was at peace at last. Boussec, Berge and Greco, however, were still alive. Boussec sat in his position playing with a handful of ants, like a child.

'Cato!' Bouchier called out again.

Cato moved along the line, and went to where Deval and Bouchier were standing.

He saw that Berge had been hit by shrapnel on the side of his face and shoulder. He sat in his position with a dazed look on his face. Greco stood waiting for Bouchier's orders. Cato joined him, but first they had to allow Deval to enjoy his victory. He was very pleased with himself. It was written all over his face. He stood silently surveying the scene with a satisfied look, as the rolling mist unfolded the extent of the shooting and the burning. It was not a pleasant sight. Cato preferred not to look. Deval turned and their eyes met. A smile appeared on Deval's lips. His chin became slightly uplifted. Nothing was said, but everything was written on their faces. On Cato's was the question, the despair, and the disgust. On Deval's was the excitement and stimulation that he had got from the battle, the flush of victory and the thought of the glory that he knew would follow. He was seeing himself as another Legion legend. He had held off and destroyed Hakim's band with only a handful of men. He had stopped Hakim at the first encounter.

'A good victory,' he said, and started to walk down the slope.

Cato felt his blood start to boil. Sasous was dead. Sasous, Hessler, Hook, and the rest, were all dead, but Deval was only concerned with his victory.

'There are still snipers on the spur, *mon*

Lieutenant,'Bouchier called to him.

Deval hesitated, and surveyed the spur and the burned plain.

'Get our dead together, Sergeant,' he ordered.

'They are not finished with us, *mon Lieutenant,*' Bouchier persisted. 'They will be back.'

'Hakim is finished,' Deval retorted. 'He has even taken his wounded. He will not be back. We have destroyed him.'

He continued on his way. Bouchier gave an angry snort of disgust.

'They are all dead,' Cato said. 'Dead – and that man is only concerned with his victory.'

'They are not finished with us yet,' Bouchier snapped. 'You might also soon be dead if you don't take care.' He looked at Greco and Cato in turn. 'Never mind the dead at the moment,' he said. 'Get a machine gun and get into position on either flank. You, Greco, take the right with Berge. Cato, take the left. Get plenty of ammunition and water and keep your eyes open. Give Vasey some as well, and the other legionnaires. They can still fire their guns. I will take up a position in the centre.'

'Aaa!... Aaa!... Aaa!'

The sudden shriek made them react. They flung themselves to the ground.

'Aaaa! Aaaa!'

The cry had come from the plain. Cato

276

looked up and saw one of Hakim's men come running out of the rolling mist from the left flank. He was a tall, khaki clad figure, brandishing a rifle in one hand and a revolver in the other. Across his chest were two bandoliers of ammunition. He was yelling and waving his arms as he darted wildly across their front. But he had an objective – Deval!

'*Mon Dieu!* He's after *le Lieutenant*,' Greco cried out.

Deval had wandered away from where they were grouped towards their left flank and was close to the wadi, but he had heard, and seen, the charging native warrior. He had his pistol in his hand. The native zigzagged towards him.

Crack! Crack! Deval fired two shots from his revolver, but the native kept on charging.

'Shoot him!' Deval shouted out. 'Shoot him!'

Cato saw Bouchier grab his machine gun. He grabbed his own rifle and hurriedly took aim. He squeezed the trigger. There was a click. It was empty! He had not reloaded it after the incident with Pedrides!

Crack! Crack! Again Deval fired. The native staggered. He had been hit. He was now only a few metres away from Deval. Deval took aim again, but no shot came from his pistol. It was almost empty! Cato watched horrified. Deval was defenceless.

277

The native warrior moved closer towards him. Deval seemed rooted to the ground.

Cato turned to Bouchier. He saw the machine gun in Bouchier's hands pointing in the direction of the charging native.

'Shoot him!' Deval yelled out. It was a cry of panic. 'Shoot him!'

The native gave another yell. Deval turned and ran.

Bang! Bang! The native fired two quick shots from his revolver. Deval lurched forward and fell to the ground on his face. The native ran up to him and fired one more shot. Then he gave a yell of triumph, and turned and ran back across the valley in the direction that he had come, into the mist.

Nothing was said. Cato stood dumbfounded. Everything had happened so quickly. Deval was dead and he had not been able to help him. But Bouchier had, he thought. Bouchier had the machine gun in his hands. Bouchier had let him be murdered!

'The gun was jammed,' Bouchier said, and held it up as if to prove his point. He looked at the two men daring them to deny his statement. He cocked the gun and cleared a cartridge from the breech. 'It was jammed,' he said again.

'Sure, Sergeant,' Greco said. 'It was jammed.'

'You disagree, Cato?' Bouchier asked.

Cato shook his head. 'No, Sergeant.'

'Get the ammunition!' Bouchier ordered, abruptly. 'Move it!'

Greco and Cato hesitated. They were both still bewildered by what had happened.

'Move it!' Bouchier snarled.

Greco moved away. So did Cato. They scrambled along the slope to where the boxes of ammunition had been dumped. Nothing was said. They opened the boxes and scrambled back along the line. They gave some ammunition to Bouchier. He was beside Berge.

'Get to your position!' Bouchier ordered, 'and keep your eyes open! I'll get Deval's body.' He gave his machine gun to Cato.

Cato scrambled back along the line and gave out the ammunition. The legionnaire who was with Sergeant Villier looked all in. He accepted the ammunition as if in a daze. Cato came to Vasey. Vasey lay with his head against the side of the wall, his eyes closed. He was in a bad way. He had lost a lot of blood. He opened his eyes as Cato joined him.

The Snake bought it,' he said, with a grimace.

'Yeah,' Cato sighed.

He gave him some ammunition.

'Can I do anything for you?'

'No, Cato. I'm O.K.'

Cato moved on. He gave some ammunition to the legionnaire in Pedrides' former position. The man took it and placed it alongside his machine gun. He also looked dazed and weary.

Suddenly a strange throbbing noise attracted Cato's attention. A cry from Greco made him turn. He saw Greco waving his arms gleefully. Then he saw why – it was a helicopter! It was sweeping towards them from the plain. His spirits immediately soared and a flood of relief surged through his body. A helicopter! They were saved! Help would be on its way! The relief inside him made him want to laugh. At first he gave a quiet chuckle and then he laughed out loud.

The helicopter came closer. It swung away from them over the valley towards Hakim's men and then came back to their position in a wide circle. Bouchier waved to it. Greco gave a cry of delight and waved his helmet.

The helicopter hovered over the ground close to where Bouchier was waving, and landed. Bouchier ran out to it. Greco joined him. Cato watched them talking to the pilot. Bouchier ordered Greco back to his position. Greco's face was bright and happy. He waved to Cato. Cato waved back. Then Cato thought of Diago and Fritz. He looked at Bouchier. What was he planning? What were they going to do? He scrambled along the line keeping his head down. He came to the helicopter. Its blades were still swirling the dust. Bouchier was in the cockpit with the pilot. They were talking over the radio. Suddenly Bouchier jumped out. Cato went up to him.

'Fritz!' he called out. 'And Diago!'

'He has only enough fuel to get back to the *poste*,' Bouchier shouted. 'He'll search for Fritz after he's refuelled.' He pulled Cato to the ground. 'Bloody snipers,' he warned.

'How many can he take?' Cato asked.

'Three or four. We'll send Berge and Sergeant Villier and his wounded. The others can still fire a gun.'

'Send Vasey as well,' Cato shouted. 'He is badly wounded.

'Vasey can still do something useful,' Bouchier shouted back.

He got up and ran back to the lines. Cato went after him and caught up with him. Again they kept low.

'Vasey needs attention badly,' Cato shouted. 'Otherwise he'll die!'

'We need his gunfire,' Bouchier retorted.

'For God's sake!' Cato pleaded. 'Get off his back. Give him a break! If Hakim comes again, we are all dead.'

Bouchier's face looked black, but Cato held his arm and wasn't letting go.

'Give him a break,' Cato pleaded again. 'He's never had one all his life.'

A shot rang out. It whined off the metal body of the helicopter.

'Get him,' Bouchier snapped, and turned away.

The two men moved quickly. Bouchier went to where Berge was crouched. Cato scrambled up to Vasey's position. Vasey was awake, but his eyes looked sunken and hazy. Cato crouched down beside him.

'Come on,' he said, hurriedly. 'You're leaving. They're flying you back to the *poste*.'

'What about you?' Vasey asked.

'They're coming back for the rest of us.'

He put his arm around Vasey to help him up. Vasey pushed it to one side.

'Hakim's men will be back,' he said.

'So let's be bloody quick,' Cato said.

'No,' Vasey said. 'I'll stay with you and the others.'

Angrily, Cato turned on him. 'Look,' he snapped, 'do as you're bloody well told. You're going on that helicopter if I have to drag you to it. You need surgery. If you don't get it soon you could die, and I don't want you to die. Do you hear? There are too many dead already.'

'Move it!' Bouchier shouted out. 'Move it!'

Greco scrambled in beside Cato.

'Come on!' he shouted.

Cato looked at Vasey. Vasey's eyes held him.

'O.K. Cato,' he said. 'Thanks.'

Cato gave a smile. He picked up a *képi* which was lying by Vasey's side and put it on Vasey's head. They carried him down the slope and got him aboard the helicopter. Berge, Sergeant Villier, and the other legionnaire, were already aboard. Vasey gave a final wave of his hand. So did the pilot. The helicopter took off. It hovered momentarily, over their position and then swung away across the plain. A fusillade of rifle fire followed it from the far side of the valley.

'It will be back,' Bouchier said. 'They will send help. If we can hold out. Captain Kubik is also on his way. Get back to your guns.'

'Sure, Sergeant,' Greco said. 'Sure. They will be back.'

His face was aglow. It was filled with the relief that Cato had felt. They dispersed. Cato went back to his own position. He saw the other legionnaire from Sergeant Villier's Section and gave him an encouraging wave. The man didn't reply. He had a look on his face that suggested he didn't fully appreciate what was going on.

'Sergeant!' a voice called out. It was Boussec. Cato turned. Boussec was standing up. 'Sergeant!' Boussec called again.

'Get your head down!' Greco shouted.

But Boussec still stood upright. He held out his hand as if to show something.

'Get down!' Bouchier shouted. 'Get down!'

'Boussec!' Greco added. 'Get down!'

But Boussec was in another world. Greco left his position to go to him.

Crack! A bullet hit Greco in the head. He fell to the ground, instantly, and lay still.

'No!' Cato groaned. 'Oh, no!'

He saw Bouchier dart across the slope to where Greco lay. Bouchier knelt down and examined Greco's body, then abruptly stood up and ran back to his own position. Greco was dead!

Cato felt a sudden burst of fury. Wildly, he picked up his machine gun and fired at the spur. The bullets sprayed the side of the mountain. He stood up and ran forward firing his gun, not aiming at anything. He was in a blind fury. Only vaguely did he see a figure fall forward and lie against one of the boulders. He continued to fire until he had spent all his rounds. Then he stood rooted to the ground.

'Get back!' Bouchier shouted. 'Get back!'

Bullets again sprayed the spur. Bouchier was now firing at it. Cato suddenly realised his vulnerability. He turned and zigzagged back across the ground. He reached his position. Bouchier also moved into it.

'You want to get yourself killed as well?' Bouchier shouted between firing a burst.

'Isn't it just a matter of time?' Cato

shouted back, and hurriedly reloaded.

Bouchier ceased firing. There were no more shots coming from the spur. He lay watching for any movement.

'Help will be on the way,' he growled.

'It won't help Greco,' Cato snapped, and watched his front. They were in the forward line. Two sub machine guns and plenty of ammunition. Behind them, higher up the slope, were two young legionnaires and Boussec, but they wouldn't be much help. Boussec was still playing with his insects like a child, and the two legionnaires were exhausted.

'Why were you so insistent about Vasey?' Bouchier asked.

Cato sighed.' You wouldn't understand,' he said. 'He's just another legionnaire to you.'

'He'll be one of the best, now,' Bouchier commented. 'He'll be good for the Legion.'

'Good for the Legion,' Cato scoffed. 'My God! Does the Legion mean so much to you?'

There was a moment's pause. Bouchier picked up his binoculars. 'It means everything to me, Cato,' he said. 'Everything. It is all I have.'

Crack! Crack! Two bullets whined into the rocks above their heads. Cato fired a return burst. More bullets smacked against their wall. The legionnaire in Pedrides' position opened up, but abruptly stopped as if his gun had jammed. There was a groan from Bouchier. Again Cato fired. He kept spraying the spur until his gun was empty. Bouchier handed him his own gun. There was blood streaming out of his gloved, right hand.

'Fire the bloody thing,' Bouchier demanded.

Cato turned and fired. Again he sprayed the rocks. He kept it up until he felt Bouchier pull him away.

'That will keep them quiet,' Bouchier shouted.

Cato lay back. He saw that Bouchier's hand was still bleeding.

'Let me bandage it,' he said.

'No,' Bouchier snapped.

'Don't be so bloody stupid,' Cato retorted. He brought out a field bandage from his tunic pocket. 'Take the glove off,' he ordered.

Bouchier hesitated.

'Take the damned thing off,' Cato said. He moved forward. Bouchier swung on him, angrily.

'Steady,' Cato intervened. 'You need it bandaged or you could lose your hand altogether.'

For a moment nothing was said.

'O.K.,' Bouchier said. 'Bandage it.'

Cato turned to face him. Bouchier held out his hand. He had removed the glove.

The bullet had gone straight through the palm. Cato hesitated. Bouchier's hand was not marked with any insignia as the men had been led to believe. His hand was small and soft, with short, slim fingers! He had been wearing padded gloves!

'What is it?' Bouchier growled.

'Nothing, Sergeant,' Cato replied.

He silently bandaged the whole hand.

'If you ever breathe a word about this,' Bouchier hissed, holding up his bandaged hand. 'I'll...'

'Don't worry,' Cato intervened. 'I won't talk.'

He turned away and watched the mountain side for any sniper. 'Deval know about it?' he asked.

Bouchier knew what Cato was referring to.

'He would know,' he growled. 'He would make it his business to find out. He was a bastard. He should never have joined the Legion. It was too good for him. The Legion doesn't need his kind. The Legion deserves only the best officers.'

And Deval didn't know just how much Bouchier loved the Legion, Cato thought. That had been his undoing. Bouchier loved the Legion so much that he was prepared to let Deval die to protect it from his kind. The gun hadn't been jammed. Bouchier had taken the opportunity to rid the Legion of

Deval. The Legion demanded something better of its officers.

Bouchier began to study the horizon with his binoculars.

'*Bon Dieu!*' he suddenly exclaimed. He handed the binoculars to Cato. 'Out on the plain,' he said.

Cato took the binoculars. The horizon bobbed about in front of his eyes. Then he saw a figure. It staggered, fell, and lay on the ground. Then it got to its feet and staggered again. It was a legionnaire!

'Fritz!' he said, his pulse quickening. 'My God! It is Fritz!'

His excitement increased. Fritz was still alive! He moved away from his gun.

'Careful!' Bouchier snapped.

'He needs help,' Cato said. 'He'll never make it.'

'He's made it so far,' Bouchier retorted. 'If you go out on the plain they'll kill you.'

'But we can't leave him,' Cato pleaded.

'They haven't seen him yet,' Bouchier said. 'If he carries on with his present course he will come to the wadi. I'll cover you. Take your gun. Keep to the wadi.'

Cato picked up his machine gun.

'Right,' Bouchier shouted. 'Go!'

Bouchier opened up and sprayed the spur of the mountain. Cato zigzagged his way to the wadi. He saw the ground spurt up in front of him as a bullet hit the ground. He slithered into the river bed. Bouchier kept up his firing. Hurriedly, Cato scrambled his way along the wadi. Suddenly two black figures appeared in front of him. He fired his machine gun from the hip. The figures fell. He ran forward and came to the point that he had fixed in his mind as his target. He stopped running and lay on the bank gasping for breath. He got his wind back and peered over the top of the wadi and saw Fritz staggering towards him. He darted over to him and dragged him behind the cover of the bank. Fritz lay face down in the soft clay. Cato grabbed his machine gun and frantically looked about him. There was no movement. He gently turned Fritz over and saw how he had suffered with the sun. His eyes were sunken and glazed and his face was covered with a dirty yellow growth. His lips were blistered and cracked and his tongue swollen. His mouth remained open as if it couldn't close. There was no look of recognition on his face. He was barely alive. Cato got his water bottle and gently poured some water into his mouth, but it stayed there. Fritz couldn't swallow.

'Fritz!' Cato urged. 'Fritz!'

He held him in his arms and the water fell out of Fritz's open mouth. He quickly brought out a piece of bandage and soaked it with water. He put it gently against Fritz's lips.

'Fritz!'

There was a flicker of movement in Fritz's eyes.

'Fritz,' he said. 'You must drink.' He squeezed the soaked bandage and let the water drip into Fritz's open mouth. Fritz made an effort. There was a cracking sound and his face twisted in pain, but he swallowed the water.

A sudden movement made Cato leave go of Fritz and grab his machine gun. He swung around – but it was Bouchier! Bouchier scrambled up to them carrying his machine gun in his left hand. He took one look at Fritz and said, 'Carry him!'

Cato picked up Fritz. Bouchier went on ahead. They made their way back along the river bed, until they were close to their position.

'Get going!' Bouchier called out and stood up and fired at the spur.

Cato zigzagged across the ground carrying Fritz and fell behind their barrier of rocks. He laid Fritz down and started firing his own gun at the spur. He saw the bullets hit the rocks. Bouchier crossed the open ground and fell in beside him. Suddenly, a scream and roar made them both hug the ground. There was a loud explosion and an aircraft screamed over their heads. Another followed and screamed over the valley. Cato looked up. They were fighters! Four French

Air Force fighters!

Whoosh! Whoosh! Two rockets left one of the fighters and screamed to the ground. They hit the mountains close to the spur. There was a thunderous explosion. Two more rockets zoomed to the ground, as another aircraft screamed up the valley. The rockets went wide of the spur, but they had the desired effect. Hakim's band started retreating across the valley. The four fighters did a wide circle and screamed up the valley again. But they didn't fire any more rockets. They let Hakim's men run for cover. Cato watched them. So did Bouchier.

'They are too damned late,' Cato said. 'They could have saved all this senseless killing. They're too late!'

Bouchier didn't answer him. He watched the retreating figures through his binoculars. He could see them going back into their mountains.

'Hakim will be back,' he said. 'The 'planes have just postponed their attack. They'll try again.'

He stood up. So did Cato. It was all over now. They could both feel it. Four aircraft and their rockets had finished the fighting. They silently looked around them. The area was strewn with dead bodies – black bodies in khaki uniforms, but all dead. Soon the vultures would be picking at their bones. Soon the heat would make their carcasses reek. Already there was a stench from the dead of the previous night. Bouchier went over to the two legionnaires who still sat in their positions behind their guns. Cato went to see Boussec. He found him still playing with his insects as if nothing had taken place.

'Look at this beetle,' Boussec said, and held up his hand. 'I've never seen one so big.'

Cato left him and went to the heap of rubble that had once been Sasous' position. He felt a heavy heart. Sasous and Pedrides had been the only persons who could have kept him in the Legion. Now they were both dead, and there was no one else. He gritted his teeth and turned away. His eyes caught the mountain peaks at the head of the valley. Beyond them was Ethiopia, he thought. Beyond them was his freedom. He had had enough of the Legion. Without Sasous he didn't want to endure it any longer. He didn't want another four years of Bouchier's type of Legion. He wanted to live again before it was too late. And he wanted to be with Jaquie. Above all else he wanted to be with Jaquie.

He took a long, deep breath and surveyed the area. He took it all in so that he would never forget it. He saw the *hole* where Pedrides still lay, and looked away. He felt no remorse about Pedrides, but he hadn't wanted to kill him. It hadn't been an eye for an eye – it had been kill or be killed. He saw the empty ammunition boxes and the uneven mounds of rocks where the men had prepared their defences. He saw the dead black native figures; the charred earth in the river bed and beyond, and the row of hastily prepared graves of the dead legionnaires. They were graves without names. They were the graves of men who had had no true identity when they had been alive. Only a legionnaire's rank, a number and an assumed name. Who they really were, only the Legion Records Department might know, but even they might not know the whole truth. But the Legion would look after them. The Legion looked after its own – and it honoured its dead. Their graves would be cared for. He turned away from them and saw Fritz. Fritz was sitting in the position that Cato had placed him, with a damp cloth across his brow and mouth. Help would soon be there, Cato thought. Fritz would get the best of attention. There was nothing more Cato could do for him.

Bouchier was getting his dead together. He carried Greco to the line of graves and placed him alongside Deval. Cato watched him and looked away. He looked over the plain. There was no sign of Hakim's men. It was over. They were returning to their hideout in the mountains, but as Bouchier had said, they would try again. It was not the end of their cause. It was just the end of that summer's fighting. Hakim was still alive, and even if he wasn't, someone else would take his place. And they would return, but Cato wasn't going to be there when he did. He had had his belly full of fighting – and of the Legion. He was ready to *travel*. But he would have to move quickly, he thought. Soon the helicopter would be back, and the reconnaissance vehicles would be on their way. He couldn't wait any longer. He hurried down the slope and picked up a canteen. It was full of water. He found a second that was also full. He also found a white *képi* and threw his steel helmet away.

A metallic click of a rifle being cocked made him freeze. He turned to see Bouchier facing him – rifle in his hand.

'Nobody deserts while I'm in charge,' Bouchier said.

'I'm still going,' Cato said. 'I'm going, Bouchier, and if you want to stop me you'll have to kill me.'

'Don't be a bloody fool,' Bouchier said. 'How far do you think you would get? The helicopter will be here any minute. There's a patrol out there.' He pointed to the head of the valley. 'Captain Kubik is on his way back. He could pick you up.'

'He'll not see me,' Cato said. 'I'll take my chances.'

'There are also Hakim's men,' Bouchier

growled, 'and the sun. You don't know the mountains. You're too tired. You'll never make it.'

Cato shook his head. 'I'm still going to try,' he said. 'The Legion is your life, Sergeant. You told me so. Well, it's not mine.'

Bouchier raised his rifle to point at Cato's chest. 'Nobody deserts on me, Cato,' he said. 'They only *travel* when they die! You're dead, Cato! Dead!'

Cato's pulse quickened. The two men stood looking at each other. Bouchier's red face, covered with a matted growth, looked like the face of the devil. And his eyes were beady and hard. Cato was uncertain. The two men stood and eyed each other.

Bouchier slowly lowered the nozzle of his rifle. 'As far as I'm concerned, Cato – you died here!' he growled. 'The others.' He moved his head indicating Boussec and the other two legionnaires. 'They don't know what is happening.'

Cato's body sagged with relief. He knew what was in Bouchier's mind. For the record, Cato had been killed in the battle. The French Government would forget all about him.

'Your equipment,' Bouchier added. 'Leave your equipment – everything!'

Cato took off his pouches and webbing. He removed them all. He stood in his combat uniform with a rifle in his hand and his water bottles.

'Give me your rifle,' Bouchier ordered.

Cato shook his head. Without his rifle he was at Bouchier's mercy.

'Don't you trust me?' Bouchier asked.

'No,' Cato replied.

The two men eyed each other again, then Bouchier's face broke into a smile. It was the first time that Cato had seen him smile.

'At least the Legion has taught you something,' Bouchier said. He picked up a haversack that was at his feet and flung it at Cato.

'There's some hard tack inside,' he said.

'Thanks,' Cato said.

Bouchier also threw him a soft, khaki bush hat. Cato caught it.

'You might need it,' Bouchier said. 'The *képi* is too conspicuous.'

Cato put the bush hat in his pocket.

Again the two men looked at each other.

'Please do one thing for me, Sergeant,' Cato said.

'What?' Bouchier asked.

'If you think Vasey is a good legionnaire,' Cato said, 'tell him. It will make him a better one.'

Bouchier gave a snort of disgust and laughed out loudly.

'Tell Vasey!' he scoffed. 'The only thing that I will tell him is not to leave his *poste* in future to interfere with two legionnaires having a duel.'

'You saw?' Cato asked. 'You saw me and Pedrides?'

'I saw nothing,' Bouchier said, 'and you are dead, Cato, and there will be a pile of rocks to prove it. Now get the hell out of here and don't you fail me. Don't you dare!'

'Sure,' Cato smiled.

He moved away. He ran quickly for a short distance and then stopped and turned. Bouchier was standing watching him. They both looked at each other. Slowly, Bouchier raised his arm and gave a wave. Cato returned the gesture and turned and faced the mountains. They looked high and impregnable, and he felt tired and weary. Perhaps they would defeat him, he thought. Perhaps he wouldn't survive the trek, but he was going to give it all he had. He would march or die. He was still a legionnaire at heart.

FIFTEEN

Cato survived the long, gruelling trek over the mountains, and eventually reached the hospital unit across the border in Ethiopia. He knew that he had survived because of the Legion and because of Jaquie. The Legion had given him the physical and mental self-discipline that he'd needed to slog it out over the mountain passes, and Jaquie had given him his inspiration and his goal. But the long trek under the blazing sun took its toll on him and as he recovered his strength under the watchful eye of the attentive medical staff of the hospital, he couldn't help but think, and wonder, at his good fortune in finding a hospital unit at the end of his ordeal.

From the hospital unit, he was driven into Addis Ababa and taken to the United States Embassy. It was late in the evening when he entered the Embassy. The journey from the relief hospital had been long and tedious, but it was over, and so was Cato's association with the Foreign Legion. He could now relax and think of the future, but he would never forget. He could never forget. He would always remember Sasous, Greco, Diago, Vasey, Fritz and the others. His time spent with them had moulded him into what he now was. He was no longer Lee Carter – civilian – he was Lee Carter – ex-legionnaire Second Class. A man who had soldiered and fought with a group of social outcasts, and he was stronger because of it. He could now live again and he was prepared to go after anything that was important to him, and that meant Jaquie. She was very important to him.

The official on duty at the Embassy did not seem surprised when he was called to attend to Cato's arrival, or with his story. He recorded the particulars and details of Cato's adventure with an air of silent efficiency that matched his youthful, but serious looking, features.

'We will have to check you out with Washington,' he said, when he had recorded all the necessary details, 'and with your bank in Philadelphia.' He looked up from his notes. 'It will only take a few days, then we shall be able to issue you with a fresh set of papers.'

'I understand.'

'In the meantime I have a reservation for you at the Park Hotel.'

Cato nodded his head in silent agreement, but his eyes were fixed on the smart, white telephone that stood on top of the polished, mahogany desk.

'I would like to make a telephone call,' he said.

'Sure,' the official replied. 'Where are you calling?'

'Djibouti.'

The official sat back in his leather, swivel chair and his serious looking face broke into a faint smile.

'Mademoiselle Chauvier?' he asked.

Cato was taken aback. 'Yes,' he said.

'A call won't be necessary,' the official said. 'She is here in Addis Ababa.'

'She is here?' Cato asked.

He got up from his chair. Jaquie was there in Addis Ababa! He heard the official saying that Djibouti was only a train journey away, but it was like hearing it through cotton wool. He was thinking of Jaquie. She was actually in the capital. He would see her that night!

'Where?' he asked.

'At your hotel.'

Cato's face lit up and he smiled broadly.

'Come on!' he said. 'Let's go.'

They left the Embassy. Cato's mind was in a whirl. Jaquie was in town! How had she known? What had she been told? The questions raced through his brain, as he was driven through the streets. He saw none of the lights of the capital, or the vehicles, the buildings, or the people. He just saw Jaquie. At the hotel the official said, 'I'll leave you to it.'

Cato ran up the steps and into the brightly

lit foyer. Jaquie was there waiting for him. He saw her straight away. She was sitting on a settee. He stopped in his tracks. She saw him and stood up. And then they were together, embracing each other, half laughing, half crying. Each thinking of the other and each knowing how the other felt.

'You knew I was alive,' Cato said. 'You knew.'

'I felt it,' Jaquie said. 'I felt it deep inside. They call it women's intuition.'

They sat on the settee facing each other.

'I also got a little help from *Le Sergeant-Chef*,' she smiled.

'*Le Sergeant-Chef*' he asked. 'Bouchier?'

'Yes, he has been promoted.'

Cato wasn't surprised.

'I went to see him,' she explained. 'I told him that I didn't believe you were dead.'

'What did he say?'

'That if I ever saw you again it would be a ghost. Then he said that if I did see such a ghost I had to tell it never to haunt him, or the Legion, again.'

Cato laughed. 'I won't,' he promised.

'He also said I had to tell the ghost that Fritz and the others would recover. Fritz is to be decorated for bravery, and Vasey is to be promoted.'

Vasey promoted! 'Well, what do you know!' Cato exclaimed. 'Bouchier has a heart after all.'

He took her hand. They looked at each other.

'It's all behind us now,' he said. 'We start from the beginning.'

'From the beginning,' she agreed.

This Large Print Book, for people
who cannot read normal print,
is published under the auspices of

THE ULVERSCROFT FOUNDATION

... we hope you have enjoyed this book.
Please think for a moment about those
who have worse eyesight than you ...
and are unable to even read or enjoy
Large Print without great difficulty.

You can help them by sending a
donation, large or small, to:

**The Ulverscroft Foundation,
1, The Green, Bradgate Road,
Anstey, Leicestershire, LE7 7FU,
England.**
or request a copy of our brochure for
more details.

The Foundation will use all donations
to assist those people who are visually
impaired and need special attention
with medical research, diagnosis
and treatment.

Thank you very much for your help.